Kim Ulrick lives on the beautiful far south coast of NSW and after a long hiatus has reconnected with her passion for storytelling. *Bad Country* is Kim's debut novel.

Kim has a Bachelor of Arts in Communication, majoring in Journalism, and she started as a junior writer and researcher with *The Australian Financial Review* in the Canberra Press Gallery.

Kim spent 30 years in the Australian Public Service working with national criminal intelligence, law enforcement agencies and departments delivering national communication strategies and policy initiatives for the Australian public. During her career, Kim engaged with Indigenous communities across northern Australia from Cairns to the Torres Strait, Darwin, the Tiwi Islands and Broome.

Kim's writing is inspired by her life experiences. When she's not writing Kim can be found playing golf, enjoying good wine and walking on the beach with her family and her beloved Kelpie. Kim's obsession with golf and wine is featured in her blog <u>Reds, Whites and Greens</u> and you can access her blog, short stories and other content at <u>kimulrickwriter.com.</u>

BAD

COUNTRY

Kim Ulrick

Contempo Publishing

652 Hogans Rd North Tumbulgum NSW 2490.
www.contempopublishing.com
Copyright © Kim Ulrick 2024.

A catalogue entry for this book is available from the National Library of Australia.

ISBN (Paperback):   978-0-6458077-6-9

Cover design and illustration by Rubi Creations Digital.
Internal design by Contempo Publishing.

Printed and distributed internationally by Ingram Spark.

First published in 2024 by Contempo Publishing.

In the spirit of reconciliation, I acknowledge the traditional custodians of Country throughout Australia and their connections to land, sea, and community. I pay respect to Elders past, present, and emerging and extend that respect to all Aboriginal and Torres Strait Islander peoples.

Author's note

The town of Wallaby Rock and all the characters in *Bad Country* are fictional, yet the story was shaped by my experiences growing up in rural New South Wales and working alongside law enforcement agencies and regional and remote communities across Australia.

There has always been a strong link between people and place. From the beauty of the natural environment to gritty urban landscapes, humans identify with the town, the city, the country they call home.

But how much does our geographical environment shape our emotions and behaviours? This connection or influence is sometimes referred to as psychogeography.

I believe evil deeds not only affect victims and their families, often for many generations, but can mark the landscape. I believe the land holds memories, just like people, and these horrific acts can seep into the soil and into the very soul of the places where they have occurred.

This book is a product of my imagination, creativity, and countless hours of hard work. It was crafted with love, passion, and dedication. Rest assured that this book was not generated by any artificial intelligence. It's a testament to the human spirit and the joy of storytelling.

www.kimulrickwriter.com

For my family,

My light in the darkness.

Prologue

Two boys chatting and laughing.

Two boys walking upriver along the gorge to the bridge.

Someone watching. Someone following.

Two boys sprawled motionless on the rocks.

Two boys she knew.

Chapter 1 – Laura

January 2020

Hidden by trees that hugged the edge of the river, Laura and her dog, Yogi, watched Sergeant Mick Peters step down the path from the bridge and duck under the chequered blue-and-white police tape.

Flies buzzed and crawled over dark stains covering the rocks near the water's edge.

Laura knew what they were.

Everything had changed since she and Yogi had taken off to the waterhole that morning for a swim.

***

It was only 9.30 am, but the shimmering haze on the horizon held the promise of yet another scorcher. After a wet start to the summer, the last week had been marked by a return to long, hot days, and the swimming hole was one of the few places to cool off, but the heat wasn't the only reason she'd come.

The pools were a tricky place to reach. Laura and Yogi had slid down the path from the cliff above, and Laura was covered in sticky sweat. The only other way in was via a longer hike upriver from the bridge and involved clambering over large rocks and logs.

Her face hot and flushed, Laura peered at the trees and bushes. No one was around. Stripping off her shorts, she stashed her battered hand-me-down mobile phone into the toes of her scuffed sneakers before stepping into the water dressed only in her underpants and a well-worn Ball Park Music t-shirt. She stood for a moment and let the gentle waves cool her feet as her toes scrunched the sand before she swam to the other side.

On the bank, she reached for a rope hanging from a large tree. Small and slender for her age, Laura remembered the pride she'd felt years ago when she could finally reach the rope without her older sister's help. Now, at eighteen, Laura was an expert at launching herself into the murky water, rife with the hidden danger of snags, submerged trees, and rocks. It was still a rite of passage for local kids to take the plunge.

A baby's cry echoed through the silence of the gully, the sound bouncing off rock walls. Laura snatched at the rope as she stumbled on the slippery bank. Heart thumping, she turned in time to catch a glimpse of a long feathery tail disappearing into the scrub. A lyrebird. The beautiful and shy creatures were masters of mimicking sounds. Breathing heavily, Laura returned her gaze to the water as she repositioned her grip.

Since her birthday in early December, everything felt different, and yet the same. Laura could legally go to the pub if she wanted to. But who with? Buy herself a car. But what with? Make her own decisions – sure – but only if her mother agreed.

And the dreams. They hadn't stopped just because she'd reached adulthood. In fact, over the last year, they'd gotten worse.

Her hair whipped her face as she swung out from the edge and then let go. Suspended in mid-air, Laura wished she had the power to freeze time, to remain carefree, young, and untroubled by dark thoughts or the difficult year that lay ahead. Clutching her knees to her chest, Laura dive-bombed to perfection.

A sharp pain shot through her foot as she clambered out for another go. Grabbing her toes, Laura muttered a colourful word she'd learned from her grandfather. Peering at the water to see what she'd stumbled over, she spied gnarled and twisted tree roots that snaked their way from the riverbank into the pool. Something was wedged between them. Intrigued, she wriggled it free, pulling out a small card. As she wiped the mud away, the outline of a football player, and what appeared to be the West Tigers' logo, appeared.

Sitting on a rock to examine her find, a loud splashing noise behind her announced Yogi had also launched himself into the refreshing water. Laura called him and then shrieked as he bounded out of the water, shaking himself dry and spraying Laura with cold droplets.

Wiping her eyes, her focus returned to the card in her hands. As she scratched away dirt from the edge of the flimsy cardboard, three letters appeared – BJT. A strangled sound escaped her as she realised this belonged to them. Without warning, the images from her dream came flooding back.

This is what jolted her awake last night, leaving her confused and uneasy.

Her restless night combined with today's warm weather had driven Laura to the waterhole. She'd hoped a swim would clear her head and seeing the river in daylight would prove it was only a horrible nightmare.

The images refused to stop. Closing her eyes once more, Laura focused all her energy on pushing them away, but it was no good. They were on constant repeat. It was like being forced to watch the trailer for a movie over and over again, but instead of Laura choosing when to stop, someone was doing it for her.

Perhaps going to the bridge would reassure her it was all a product of what she hoped was an over-active imagination. Pulling on her shorts and shoes and shoving the card in her back pocket, Laura followed the bank upriver, toward the bridge.

As she got closer, Laura could hear a commotion. Stepping carefully so as not to make noise, she spied people swarming up and down the opposite bank. She hesitated for a moment before moving behind the trees to silently view the activity around her. Bubbles of anxiety swirled in her stomach as she drew Yogi close.

Laura saw Sergeant Peters, head of the local police force, make his way down the path. Only a few weeks ago, Sergeant

Peters had stopped her as she drove home on her Ps, congratulating her on passing her driving test and reminding her about needing to pay close attention when navigating rough country roads.

Laura saw his shoulders move up and down as if he were sucking in long, deep breaths. He headed for the officers taking photos and collecting evidence.

Laura covered her nose as the pungent, tangy scent of blood wafted across the hot air to her hiding spot. Her eyes were drawn to the rocks, and she pictured her friends lying there, blood pooling around their heads. She smothered a sob with her hand. The noise startled a lizard that darted out from the trees and scurried to the shelter of a nearby boulder.

Keep it together, she told herself, her pulse galloping.

Laura recognised her neighbour Jacquie, Wallaby Rock's chief gossip and self-proclaimed town blogger, peering over the bridge and chatting with other locals. Jacquie would soon broadcast the gory news across town, including detailed descriptions of the reactions and views of everyone she saw and spoke to.

Sergeant Peters glanced up at the bridge where reporters and television crews had joined Jacquie and the local townspeople – his head dropped. After a few seconds, he put his hands on his hips and stood with his eyes shut before looking out across the river and letting fly with a choice swear word. Laura sank back behind a bush and held her breath, but in the next instant, the brawny officer turned on his heels and attacked the climb to the top.

Biting down on her bottom lip, Laura fingered the footy card in her back pocket, making sure it was still there. Was this happening?

While keen for a closer view, she didn't want to be quizzed about what brought her to the bridge. The police had set up barriers on the opposite side to stop people from coming down. They didn't want anyone poking around the riverbank and interfering with their investigation. If they spotted her on the other side, there'd be questions … questions she didn't want to answer. She pictured the look of incredulity that would grow on the face of Sergeant Peters if she told him her dream had led her there. She could lie and say she'd decided to head to the bridge after swimming because the path was easier to climb, but she didn't think testing her acting ability in front of the town's senior police officer was a smart idea. And thinking about what her mother would say if she were interviewed by the police about a potential homicide gave her another reason to hesitate.

Homicide? That's how they described a murder, wasn't it? The word rattled around in her brain like a ball pinging off the sides of the pinball machine her father kept in the shed. Shaking her head, Laura tried to still the noise and a wave of sadness washed over her. She'd seen enough. It was best to stay quiet and

wait for the right moment before heading back to the waterhole
and then home.

Chapter 2 – The gorge

Leaving the crime scene, Laura and Yogi made their way back along the river before climbing the steep ascent to the towering cliff that stood guard over the gorge. Inching closer, she dangled her legs over the edge before leaning back and closing her eyes to listen to the wind moving through gum trees overhead, trying to shake the feeling of dread that had been building for days. The constant hum of cicadas and the sharp, sweet smell of eucalyptus filled her senses, and for a moment, she was at peace with the bush, the bloodied river rocks no longer top of her mind.

This was Laura's special place. Growing up, it was where she would come after school, on weekends, and during holidays to escape, calm her mind, and reset her mood.

She visited the gorge in her waking hours and in her dreams, dreams that had turned dark over the last twelve months, like her 'falling dream'. Trapped on her bed and descending to the bottom of the deep chasm, blurry faces flashed by and screams pierced her ears. But worst of all was the 'Shadow Man' who stalked her, often appearing in the doorway to her bedroom. He never spoke; his presence was enough to fill her with fear.

Laura filled her lungs and then breathed out. The soft hiss of air being exhaled combined with the sound of rustling leaves. Her mind calmed. She caressed the sandstone beneath her fingers. Warmth oozed from its rough surface, flowing through her hands and into her body. The rock pulsed with heat. With life. With power.

Opening her eyes, she scanned the landscape before her: the wombat holes Yogi loved to sniff, the walls of jagged sandstone, and the green ribbon of ferns and thick undergrowth that followed the river below. She was at home here in the bush. But maybe, she thought, as she felt the sting of hot sun on her face, she should've listened to her mother and worn a hat.

Laura didn't look her age. On her eighteenth birthday, her older sister, Sarah, had driven them to Sydney to spend the weekend with one of their aunts. All three had gone to a trendy nightclub, but Laura had been refused service, the bar staff convinced her licence was fake. She was often mistaken for a much younger person, but the incident rankled her. Laura had fair skin and a mass of freckles; her bright blue eyes were the only feature she considered pretty. She had muscular legs, a formidable left hook, and a temper to match the auburn hair that draped in a messy ponytail down her back.

Laura was part of a large extended family; her mother, Jeannie, was one of nine girls. Henry, her father, was one of eleven children. Laura's uncles had spent long hours, since the time she could walk, teaching her to box – a skill Laura had used on the boys in primary school when they tried to pull her hair or call her names. She became a regular visitor to the principal's office, and her parents were told she needed to find ways of resolving conflict that didn't involve using her fists.

Laura grinned to herself when she thought of the Jones brothers, who had delighted in tormenting her and Sarah on the school bus. After months of putting up with their behaviour, the Murray sisters had had enough. Laura had given one brother a bloody nose while Sarah had given the other a fat lip. When the boys complained to the bus driver, he'd told them they got what they deserved, but the boys' parents complained to the school. Laura's mother forced her and Sarah to apologise to the boys to avoid a school suspension. Laura didn't like bullies, and when it came to managing them, she preferred to do it herself.

Laura's family lived with her grandparents, Grace and Jack, on a dairy farm at Wallaby Rock in regional New South Wales. The town was named after a large sandstone rock that resembled a crouching wallaby. It stood in the park next to the town hall. The Murray farm had been theirs for many generations, and it backed onto public bushland that Laura loved.

****

Okay, her face was starting to prickle and burn now, and Yogi was nosing a wombat hole, his front paws moments away from digging. She whistled, and the German shepherd-labrador cross bounded over, tongue lolling out the side. *Silly dog*, she thought, but she loved him so much her heart almost burst. Six years ago, Laura had convinced her father to rescue Yogi from the shelter, and while her mother complained about the strays Laura brought home, Yogi was special. He not only knew what she was thinking, Yogi had a secret. The dog was a kleptomaniac; he often stole groceries from the neighbours – his favourite was fresh bread. Yogi would wait until the delivery truck had gone, then collect his booty and bury the loaves in the backyard. And he didn't stop at bread. Yogi once came home with a velvet skirt and one work boot. Her father, Henry, had laughed. 'What good is one boot, Yogi?' The next day, the other boot appeared.

Yogi licked her cheek, and she hugged him, burying her face in his fur. He had been her constant companion and best friend through the tumultuous and lonely years of high school. The darkness that had consumed her all day began to ebb away.

'Let's go, boy,' Laura said as Yogi cocked his head to one side as if to say, 'About time.' Yogi didn't need to speak to make himself understood.

'Time for lunch,' Laura added, getting to her feet. Yogi barked his agreement and led the way home.

Chapter 3 – Mick

'What are those people doing here?' Sergeant Mick Peters' index finger stabbed the air, pointing to nosy locals milling around the police cars. What began as a couple of interested onlookers who'd turned up shortly after the ambulance arrived had swelled to more than a dozen people. The group had watched in morbid fascination and recorded the police officers carrying two body bags from the rocks below the bridge, loading them into the back of the ambulance.

Even after five years stationed at Wallaby Rock, Mick was still getting used to small-town life.

When a media van with a television logo plastered on the side pulled up, and the crew joined those loitering near the bridge, along with the town's biggest stickybeak and blogger, Mick sighed at the circus.

In his mid-fifties, and despite the tell-tale signs of middle-age spread starting to show beneath the uniform that bulged across his stomach, the policeman still had a commanding presence. He turned to Senior Constable Bob Fowler. 'Bob, go and tell those jokers they'll get their briefing in half an hour and not before. And for God's sake, tell those locals to get back.'

Running his fingers under his sweaty collar, Mick knew it was going to be a hot one. It was barely 11 am, and the temperature was already in the mid-thirties – the oppressive heat wasn't helping his mood. This case had him rattled. He didn't understand why. It wasn't the first time he'd had to deal with unexpected, tragic, and gruesome events.

Mick was at the tail end of his police career after moving his family from Sydney to the slower pace and small-town vibe of Wallaby Rock. He'd grown tired of dealing with the city's drug addicts and, worse still, the scum who supplied the stuff that hooked young kids, ruined their lives, and tore apart families.

Fifteen years working the inner-city beat had been enough. Bikies and crime gangs cropped up all over the place, like weeds in a garden. Getting on top of them fast was the key to success. And most people knew better than to get him started on lawyers and the justice system that let scumbags go with a gentle reprimand, only for them to reappear in court months later, having committed the same crimes. The job was tough, and Mick had lost too many mates to its pressures. His partner, Peter, was one of them. A friend since they'd joined the force together, Peter had never talked about his feelings or shared what he was going through. Instead, he'd signed out his firearm, like he did every day, and sat in the patrol car for thirty minutes before taking his own life. He'd told Mick he was going to get them a coffee. Afterwards, Mick spiralled into depression, and his wife, Shirley, presented him with an ultimatum. Get out of Sydney or she'd walk.

Until now, the most serious issues Mick had dealt with at Wallaby Rock were drunk drivers, teens smoking weed, and domestic violence.

But he hadn't expected this, blocking off one of the southbound traffic lanes so they could safely investigate two unusual deaths. That sort of thing didn't happen in his sleepy town. Yet here he was, watching a car crawl by, the ogling driver craning his neck.

'Bloody rubberneckers,' Mick muttered, turning to peer into the gorge himself, grasping the railing. His thoughts returned to the conversation he'd had earlier in the morning when he broke the news to the father of the boys who were now on their way to the coroner's office.

***

Arthur Thompson had wept, head in his hands, when Mick broke the news that his twin sons, Benny and Jordy, were dead. 'I want to see my boys, Mick. Bring them home,' Arthur whispered.

'Of course, Arthur.' Mick paused, touching the man's arm and searching for the right words. 'But they'll need to stay with us for a while until a full examination is conducted, to determine the cause of death. And we'll need you to come to the station to give a proper statement and answer some routine questions.'

Arthur's grief turned to anger as he pushed Mick's hand away. 'I told you they were missing. You didn't believe me! And now you think I had something to do with this, don't you? You lot are unbelievable!'

'Arthur, c'mon. I never said that, and they're young men who are known to skip school and take off now and then …' Mick faltered as Arthur stared him down.

'My kids not worth the effort, hey?' Mick shook his head and opened his mouth to speak, but Arthur cut him off. 'Nah, don't try and tell me any different. I know what people say about me and what they think of my family. And I'll tell you something – my boys wouldn't have been mucking around on that bridge. They know better.'

'Why? What do you mean?' asked Mick, his voice sharper than he intended.

'My kids wouldn't hang out there. That's all you need to know,' Arthur said, slamming the door in Mick's face.

***

Shuffling his feet, Mick stared at the rocks below, wishing he could turn back time. His knuckles turned white as he gripped the railing harder. A wave of nausea threatened to overwhelm him, but he pushed it down, along with the guilt he would have to live with for not listening to Arthur. Shaking his head, he made his way to the end of the bridge, cautiously picking his way down the sloping dirt track. Huffing and puffing, he reached the bottom of the gorge where the river slowed to a narrow creek. Mick greeted the forensic officers who were still taking photos, examining the spot where the bodies had been found and collecting evidence.

A council worker who lived in town made the grim discovery at 7.30 that morning while checking on the river's water quality and levels. Although shaken, the man had not touched the bodies or disturbed the scene and had at once called the police.

Mick knew Benny and Jordy were not bad kids. They were well-known for ditching school, and with a couple of underage drinking offences and official warnings for driving without a licence, they were typical young men who pushed the boundaries and thought they were bulletproof. They were also rock stars in the football community, and neither lad had a history of depression or self-harm. The most rational explanation was the brothers had fallen from the bridge while fooling around … except for the injuries and position of the bodies.

Hearing a sound near the trees to his left, Mick turned in time to see a small lizard scamper to the safety of a large boulder. Mick clicked his tongue and returned his gaze to the crime scene, his eyes tracing the eighty or so metres up to the bridge.

Assuming Arthur was right, the only explanation was foul play. He hoped the full toxicology report would hold the answer.

But he'd have to bring Arthur in, find out where he was last night and check out any alibis. Mick didn't believe Arthur was capable of killing his children, or anyone else, but he'd heard the rumours too. Mick knew he needed to silence them. The last thing he needed were ill-informed vigilantes seeking justice.

Hands on his hips, Mick squeezed his eyes closed, hoping to wipe yet another horrific crime scene from his mind. A moment later, he opened his bloodshot eyes and looked across the gently gurgling river.

He'd spoken to the forensics team. They'd identified the cause of death as severe trauma to the skull, and while there were scratches on their arms and legs, the boys hadn't broken any bones or sustained any other life-threatening injuries. In Mick's mind, the facts didn't add up. He'd heard whispers of a drug dealer moving into town. Could this be a deal gone wrong? Considering the walls of the gorge and the thick bushland that surrounded the area, it would be easy to hide tonnes of drugs. Maybe the twins had gotten involved in illegal steroids to bulk up for footy? In the end, it was all speculation until the autopsy results came through.

He felt the responsibility of the investigation weighing him down as he made his way up the path to the road.

Chapter 4 – Laura

'Hi, Gran,' Laura called as she entered the old sprawling farmhouse.

'Hands,' Grace replied.

Laura rolled her eyes and headed for the bathroom. In eighteen years, the routine has never changed. Laura was always disappearing for hours on end and turning up at mealtime. After washing her hands, she took her spot at the large table that occupied most of the kitchen. 'What's for lunch?'

'Ham and mustard sandwiches,' Grace responded.

Laura pulled a face. 'Again?' she moaned.

'With an attitude like that, young lady, you can help yourself to bread and butter,' Grace retorted.

They both smiled before Laura turned away.

Now in her sixties, Grace Murray was still a striking woman, with dark wavy hair greying at the temples and shaped into a bob that framed blue-grey eyes. The older woman was always well-presented, unlike Laura, who believed in the bare minimum when it came to personal grooming. Grace insisted you should always have your face on – meaning make-up – and always say please and thank you. 'No need to let standards slip, just because you live on a farm,' she'd tell Laura.

Laura didn't see the sense in wasting time trying to make herself look pretty. She figured nothing would help, and it wasn't like there were a lot of guys around to impress anyway. No guys who were interested in her, anyway.

She could still remember the excitement she felt when she was fifteen and was asked to hang out with a good-looking boy from Wallaby Rock High at the local dance. He'd bought her a soft drink and spent time chatting with her before asking her to meet him behind the hall. She'd snuck out, hoping to experience her first kiss, and overheard him around the corner laughing and talking to his mates, saying how easy it had been to convince the crazy girl that he was interested in her. Laura had tripped over in her rush to get away and spent the rest of the night stemming blood from a cut under her chin as she hid in the toilet. She vowed never to go to another dance.

Laura sniffed the air. Apple and cinnamon. 'Can I smell teacake?' She turned to the kitchen bench where a cake sat cooling on a wire rack.

'Lunch first,' her grandma stated in her do-as-you're-told voice. 'If I let you start now, there'd be no cake left for anyone else.'

Laura's mother, Jeannie, had taken Sarah to visit her piano teacher in town. Sarah was an accomplished pianist and had been accepted into university to study music. Her teacher was giving her some final tips and practice before she began her studies. Laura's father and grandfather were out working the farm.

On any other day, Laura would have cherished time alone with Gran. Today, she was struggling to act like everything was normal.

She could pretend she'd stumbled across the crime scene while walking with Yogi. But Gran had a way of extracting the truth, a knack for getting inside her head. It was like her she possessed a superpower, like Superman's x-ray vision, and Laura had no desire to relive her dreams and visions.

When she was thirteen, her mother had taken her to see a woman, who turned out to be a child counsellor, to help Laura overcome what Jeannie described as 'night terrors' and 'unusual behaviour'. Laura hated the sessions; they made her feel like she was defective. She was tired of the other kids looking at her like she was different and saying things about her behind her back. She'd convinced everyone, including the counsellor, that the bad dreams had stopped. She then proceeded to retreat further into herself. Only Sarah knew the truth. If Jeannie found out now, Laura worried she would have her committed.

And Laura had other things to concentrate on.

It was January 2020, the height of the Australian summer, and when school went back, she'd be starting Year 12, her final year at Saint Benedict's, an all-girls Catholic college around an hour's bus ride from the farm.

Laura's reputation for being weird had followed her to high school. Sometimes the things Laura saw in her dreams would invade her waking hours, coming back to haunt her at the most inconvenient times. She couldn't control when this happened, and it didn't help when she'd stare into the distance, unresponsive to people around her as images and feelings overwhelmed her. Laura had tried to act more normal, to chip away at the image her peers had formed of her, but like chewing gum stuck to the bottom of a shoe, no matter what she tried, some of the sticky residue remained.

Over the last six years, she'd only made a couple of friends. Anyone who'd considered hanging out with her had been scared off by Olivia Hansen, or Liv, the mayor's daughter and head bully of the school. Liv described herself as an 'emerging influencer' who liked to tell anyone in earshot how many new followers she had each day. Liv delighted in taunting Laura, often filming her and editing the footage to make her look like a total idiot and then distributing it on her Snapchat and TikTok accounts. Laura held on to the slim possibility that Liv may have matured and would leave her alone for her final year, but then again, Liv hadn't shown any sign of growing a heart. Laura's parents would be mortified to learn what the cruel teenager and her cronies had done to their daughter, but as her parents didn't have social media accounts, they were unaware of what Laura was going through. Laura preferred it that way. She liked to fight her own battles.

Many of the classmates from her old primary school had moved to Wallaby Rock High, including Joanna, who'd been

Laura's closest friend. They were still mates but had grown apart over the last six years, only catching up on weekends and holidays and for training sessions.

Running was important to Laura. It was an outlet for her frustration and her competitiveness; it gave her a purpose and a way to keep the dark thoughts at bay. The counsellor she'd seen when she was younger had encouraged her to exercise and spend time in nature as a way of levelling her emotions and tiring herself out each day. It was the only positive thing Laura had taken from their sessions.

She dreamed of making the state and even the national team. Perhaps then she'd be someone others would admire and want to be with. Joanna had always been better than her – she was a state champion – and training with her and her younger brothers, Benny and Jordy, inspired Laura to strive to be faster and stronger. She also felt like less of a misfit when she hung out with them.

Since starting high school, her father had promised to train her, but the farm kept him busy, and since the deregulation of the dairy industry many years ago, the family had battled to stay afloat. Laura could see he was struggling to keep the farm from going under. She didn't want to add to the pressure he was already dealing with.

Laura hadn't told her family she was training with the Thompsons. Joanna had a reputation around town for drinking, getting into fights, and bad-mouthing anyone who challenged her. Jeannie would raise her eyebrows and shake her head whenever anyone spoke of the latest exploits of Joanna Thompson. The twins were also known to get into trouble, but their talent at football and cheeky manner made them loveable larrikins, while Joanna was labelled a wild child. But more than that, Laura couldn't bear to see the guilty look on her father's face, a look that said he'd let her down. The farm sucked all his time, money, and energy. So, she'd kept her training and ongoing friendship a secret. A secret only Sarah knew.

Chapter 5 – Grace

Grace eyed her granddaughter over the rim of her teacup. Most days, Laura chattered away like a magpie. Something was off. Grace knew Laura had always struggled to fit in with people her own age; she preferred the company of Yogi and wandering the bush by herself to hanging out with friends or browsing the internet. Laura was what her Irish mother would have called 'an old soul' – a *síceach*.

As a child, what came out of Laura's mouth sometimes was best described as insights from a wise old woman. Like the time Laura had patted their neighbour Jacquie's arm, telling the older woman not to be sad because she couldn't have children. At the time, Laura was only five.

Grace believed the gift of sight was strong on her mother's side of the family, the O'Briens. Jack's family, the Murrays, had a strong Scottish-Irish connection, having come to Australia as convicts two hundred years ago. But it was Grace who upheld the old Irish customs. Her parents, Bridget O'Brien and Peter Malone, had emigrated to Australia in the 1950s as part of the post-war immigration boom, searching for a better life. Grace was the first of the Malones to be born in Australia.

Some traditions Grace kept alive were common practices in the Murray household, like throwing salt over your left shoulder three times to ward off bad luck or leaving out a saucer of milk on Saint Patrick's Day for the little people. Grace would also read tea leaves for close family and friends. She took the responsibility and the readings seriously, not knowing if the news was going to be good or bad.

At the table, Laura swallowed the last of her sandwich, her big, blue eyes pleading.

'Oh, alright. One piece for us both,' said Grace.

In a blink, Laura was at the bench, cutting off enormous chunks of teacake. She returned to the table. Cheeks bulging, she handed her grandmother a generous slice and took a second piece to the table for herself.

Grace was in the middle of spreading butter to every corner of the cake when the phone rang. She rushed to the adjacent lounge room and lifted the cordless phone from its charging station to her ear.

'Hello. This is Grace,' she said in refined tones, lowering herself onto a well-worn armchair. 'Oh, hello, darl.'

Chapter 6 – Laura

As Gran settled in for a chat with one of her children, extended family, or friends, Laura slathered butter on her second chunk of still-warm teacake. About to take a huge bite, Gran's sharp intake of breath stopped her.

'No, I hadn't heard,' Grace was saying. 'Where were they?' she asked, lowering her voice.

Laura pretended to focus on the important job of eating, but her eyes never left Gran's face. As the minutes stretched on, the lines on Grace's forehead deepened. Making the sign of the cross, Grace said, 'Oh, that's awful. Thanks for letting me know, Jacquie. Right, thanks.'

Laura knew whenever Gran blessed herself, it was serious.

Grace sat in her armchair, holding the phone for what felt like a long time before returning to the table. Laura stared at her grandmother, watching every movement and waiting for confirmation that everything she'd dreamt was true.

The clatter of Grace's teacup as she placed it back on the saucer reverberated in the silent kitchen. Grace lifted her head and grasped Laura's hand.

'That was Jacquie. There's been an incident at the bridge. Two boys have died. It's Benny and Jordy Thompson. The police are expected to make a statement soon, confirm it's them, but everyone is saying it's the twins.'

Laura stared at Gran, but instead of the gentle concern etched on her grandmother's face, all Laura could see were images of the boys sprawled on the rocks. With an enormous effort, she brought herself back to the present, and her thoughts turned to Joanna. Oh God, what would her friend be going through?

'That's terrible, Gran. Poor Mr Thompson and his daughter …' Laura couldn't finish her sentence.

Grace patted her arm. 'I know, darl. It's dreadful. Especially after their mother …' Grace's voice trailed off, and this time, it was Laura who squeezed her grandmother's hand. 'Jacquie said some of the women in town are preparing meals for the family. I'll make one of my casseroles. It's the least I can do.'

Laura nodded, and they cleared the table. Gran knew Laura had gone to school with the Thompson children, but she didn't know about the depth of her connection to the boys and their sister. Grace was unaware they all ran together.

Benny and Jordy had been annoying little kids at first, always getting in the way of Laura and Joanna's plans, but Laura, who had no brothers, enjoyed their teasing and cheeky banter. Sisterly affection had blossomed into something more substantial as the boys' muscular and athletic bodies filled out.

Laura dried the dishes Grace handed to her and placed them on the bench without thinking as she stared out the kitchen window to the paddocks and bush beyond. Was there something she could have done? Should she have told her family about her dreams this morning or talked to the police? And what about Joanna? She needed to talk to her, to check in on her friend. Sunlight streamed in through the kitchen window, and yet, Laura shivered.

Grace carved two large portions of teacake, asking Laura to take them to her father and grandfather.

Laura almost sprinted to the door. She couldn't stay inside a moment longer.

Chapter 7 – Grace

After Laura strode away, Yogi by her side, Grace returned to the lounge room and her armchair, picked up the phone, and dialled Jacquie's number.

'Jacquie, it's Grace. I'm free to talk now. Tell me more.'

Jacquie revealed she had gone to the pub to place some bets, and Jim, the publican, had told her that a council worker had found the twins' bodies early that morning under the bridge that spanned the gorge. Arriving at the scene, Jacquie saw the bodies being loaded into the ambulance and police officers collecting evidence by the river. What was not clear was whether the boys had fallen or jumped from the bridge, if it may have been a suicide pact or, even worse, if they had been pushed. Some people were already asking where their father had been at the time of the boys' deaths.

When Grace hung up, she sat in the empty lounge room for several minutes, processing all she'd heard. Rising from her chair, she walked down the long, narrow hallway to her bedroom. Pulling open the drawer of her antique dressing table, she took out her rosary beads and glanced up at the large painting of Saint Patrick that dominated the room. With a fierce expression on his face, Saint Patrick was standing on a rock at the edge of the sea, driving the snakes from Ireland. The painting had belonged to her mother, who often reminded Grace she should never forget her heritage and should pray to their patron saint for guidance when needed.

Grace knelt by the bed and started a rosary, moving the beads through her fingers while her lips moved soundlessly to the rhythm of the prayers. The familiar ritual calmed her, and she offered up an extra prayer to Saint Patrick for the souls of the two boys.

Twenty minutes later, the low thrum of an engine grew louder as a car made its way down the long drive. The squeak of rusty hinges was followed by quick footsteps, and her granddaughter Sarah rushed into the kitchen, planting a kiss on her cheek.

'Hi, Gran,' Sarah said.

'How was your lesson?' Grace asked.

'Okay,' said Sarah, adding in a whisper, 'Miss Patricia gave me heaps to work on. She expects me to top the class at uni, but don't tell Mum.'

Grace smiled at the granddaughter who was like a mini version of her. At nineteen, Sarah was tall with dark curly hair cropped in the latest short style that framed a pretty face and light grey eyes. Laura, on the other hand, was a good mix of her mother, Jeannie, and her father, Henry. Laura was shorter and fairer like her mother but had the trademark blue Murray eyes. Her auburn hair was a throwback to her Irish heritage. Laura might not look as much like her, but Grace felt the young woman was an O'Brien through and through.

'Sarah, can you help me with the shopping, please,' called Jeannie from the front door.

'Yep, sorry, Mum,' Sarah said, running off to help.

Grace rose from her chair at the kitchen table and took her dishes to the sink. Reaching for the tap, she peeked inside her teacup. Narrowing her eyes, she turned it to the left, then to the right. It was unmistakable – a cross. An omen of suffering. Of death. Leaning against the bench, she let the water wash away the message she felt sure she was meant to see.

'Did you hear about the two boys?' Jeannie asked her mother-in-law as she hoisted three bulging bags onto the kitchen table. Jeannie was a petite, fair woman with an elfin face, dark hair, large blue eyes, and long dark lashes. Despite her slight frame, Grace knew Jeannie was a strong woman and a disciplinarian when it came to her two granddaughters.

'Yes, Jaquie called. It's terrible.' Grace composed herself before turning to face Jeannie.

They stopped talking as Sarah came in, depositing bags on the table before returning to the car for more.

'Poor Arthur! His sons … gone,' Jeannie whispered. 'Sarah was with Miss Patricia the whole time, so I managed to keep her away from the gossip, but it must be all over the town by now.'

'Sarah's mature enough to deal with this, you know,' Grace reassured Jeannie.

Jeannie nodded. 'I know they're not little girls anymore, but I don't want Sarah worrying about this, not when she's about to move to Sydney, and Laura … You know Laura. She feels and thinks too much. She has a big year to get through. I don't want her … distracted.'

'Too late. Laura heard me on the phone to Jacquie,' Grace confessed.

'What? Oh no. That's not good. I'd better tell Sarah. It's not fair if she's the last to know.'

Grace nodded as Sarah came in with three more bags, huffing as she plonked them on the table. 'That's all of them, Mum,' she said, wiping her palms on her jeans.

Jeannie pulled a chair out from the kitchen table. 'Sarah, sit down for a moment. I need to tell you something.'

Sarah perched on the edge of the seat, her eyes darting from Jeannie to Grace. 'What's wrong?'

'There's been a tragedy at the bridge. Two boys were found dead this morning. It's Arthur Thompson's sons.'

'The twins? Benny and Jordy?' Sarah stammered. 'I don't believe it!'

'I know you and Laura went to school with them. I thought you should know. I expect it will be all over the news later,' Jeannie finished.

'Does Laura know?' Sarah asked, and Grace nodded her reply.

Sarah continued to sit at the table, her hands loose in her lap, staring out the window.

'Why don't you see what your father and grandfather are up to? It's almost milking time,' Grace gently suggested.

'Sure,' Sarah muttered as she pushed her chair back and ambled in a daze to the door.

They listened for squeaky hinges and the thud of a door closing before Jeannie resumed their earlier conversation. 'Maybe they were mucking around and fell,' she said.

'I hope that's all it was,' Grace said, touching the small gold cross that lay on a delicate chain against her chest.

Chapter 8 – Laura

As she made her way through the paddocks, searching for her father and grandfather, Laura mulled over what she'd seen at the bridge, the phone call, and Gran's confirmation that her friends were indeed gone. Around her, the bush was quiet; even the birds and insects had taken refuge from the sudden onset of summer. The silence only made the thoughts in Laura's head louder.

Her father and grandfather had finished repairing a boundary fence and were packing everything into the back of a Holden ute that had seen better days when Laura spied them.

Having been out since early that morning, Laura guessed they were unaware of what had happened. She waved flies away as she joined them. 'Hi, Dad. Hi, Grandad.'

'Laura, where's your hat? You shouldn't need to be told. You're old enough to know better,' grumbled Henry as he leaned over to pick up the last of the tools.

'Sorry, Dad,' Laura mumbled.

Henry glanced at Jack. Laura usually took any opportunity to get in a quick retort or cheeky response.

'I brought you a treat.' Laura retrieved two large and squashed pieces of teacake wrapped in baking paper from her pockets.

'You saved me some!' Henry smiled. 'For that, we'll give you a ride home. But first, cake!'

As they chewed, Laura piped up. 'Dad, Grandad, have you heard about what happened this morning? At the bridge?' She watched their faces closely to gauge their reactions.

It was Jack who responded first. 'No. What happened, Laura?' he asked as he opened the car door.

'Two boys were found there. Dead. Gran said the police are going to say something about it soon. It will be on the news tonight.' Saying it out loud made it more real, and Laura shivered in the bright summer sun.

'Who was it, Laura?' Henry asked. Laura noticed the lines around his eyes deepening as they always did when he was worried.

'Benny and Jordy Thompson,' Laura whispered.

'Oh God. Poor Arthur. His only sons.' Jack's voice broke. He looked like a tough old bushie, but Laura knew her grandfather was a gentle soul who loved his family and his community.

Laura nodded, turning away to wipe tears from her cheeks that she couldn't hold in any longer. Henry pulled her into a hug. 'Oh, love. There's not much we can do but say a prayer for the boys. Let's get back, get the milking done, and see if there's any more news.'

Calling for Yogi to join her, Laura clambered onto the ute tray and hung on tight as her grandad negotiated the rough cattle tracks that wound through the paddocks.

Jack parked the rusty vehicle beside the milking shed. Sarah was sitting on the gate to the milking yard, waiting for them.

Before Sarah could start another conversation about the death of the twins, Henry cut in. 'Let's get the milking done as quick as we can. Why don't you give us a hand, girls?'

Laura jumped down and whistled to Yogi, who started herding the black-and-white dairy cows towards the milking yard. Laura loved the placid nature of the Friesians and fell asleep each night listening to the sound of their soft lowing.

Sarah opened the gate, and the cows, who knew the routine, ambled through the yard and into the milking shed. The four of them shepherded the cows into stalls where they attached suckers to their teats while the cows enjoyed a bucket of grain. The milk was then sucked into a large vat where it was pasteurised before going to market. Once milked, each cow received a gentle slap on the backside before moving to the outer paddocks. Yogi helped them along.

After all the cows were milked, they cleaned and sterilised the equipment and hosed out the shed. Cows produced tonnes of milk, but they also pooped a lot. Using a shovel, Laura scooped cow dung into a pile to be later sold as fertiliser. The smell never bothered her; her grandad called it 'farmers' perfume'.

After cleaning up, Jack and Henry retired to the lounge room to watch the evening news with a couple of beers while Sarah and Laura finished setting the table.

The iconic music that heralded the start of the nightly news bulletin echoed through the house, and Grace, Jeannie, Sarah, and Laura rushed in. Henry turned up the television as the news presenter began.

'Better known for farms and pristine bushland, the town of Wallaby Rock has been shocked today by the discovery of two bodies. We cross now to John Gordon at the scene.'

An officious-looking young male reporter appeared on the screen. The bridge and part of the gorge were visible in the background. Laura and her family sat in stunned silence. This was their hometown on the nightly news – it was surreal.

'It was here under this bridge, which leads to the small town of Wallaby Rock, that the bodies were found,' the reporter said.

'Police have released the names of the victims. They are sixteen-year-old twins Benny and Jordy Thompson – teenagers from the local area, both with promising futures in rugby league.'

The news report crossed to footage of Sergeant Mick Peters, who said: 'It is not yet clear if death was accidental, and at this stage, foul play has not been ruled out. Our investigations are continuing.'

Images of the twins in their footy uniform and footage of the local pub, railway station, park, town hall, and shops reinforced the location of the tragedy while the voice of the reporter played over the top.

'There is no doubt this will be a big blow to this small and tight-knit community.'

The picture switched back to the reporter.

'John Gordon, National Nightly News.'

***

Laura was quiet during dinner, pushing her peas around with her fork and making patterns in her mashed potato. She felt Jeannie counting her every bite. Laura forced herself to finish her peas before taking her plate to the kitchen.

Sarah followed her, closing the door behind them as they entered the bedroom that they'd shared all their lives. They hadn't had a chance to talk in private all afternoon.

'Are you alright, Laura?' Sarah asked as she perched on the edge of the bed next to her sister. Sarah knew Laura was still friends with Benny and Jordy and their sister, Joanna. She also knew Laura often snuck off to their place. Laura was grateful her sister protected her secrets.

'You know the bridge is high. They could have fallen,' Sarah said, trying to reassure her younger sister.

Twisting her hands in her lap, Laura stammered, 'I knew … I knew it was Benny and Jordy … before the police said anything.' She stopped short of telling Sarah the boys had not been on the bridge. Of confiding that she thought their deaths were no accident.

Sarah placed a hand on Laura's shoulder. 'Did you dream it?'

Laura nodded. 'Last night. Then this morning I saw the same pictures from my dream – again – in my head. And I found this, at the waterhole,' Laura pulled the tattered footy card out of her back pocket. 'It belonged to them.'

Sarah pulled her into a hug. 'I think you should tell Mum and Dad.'

'No!' Laura lifted her head from Sarah's chest. 'Don't tell them. Whether I saw anything or found something, it doesn't change what happened. It won't … bring them back.'

Over the years, Sarah had often been woken by Laura tossing and talking in her sleep. When later describing it to Laura, Sarah said it was like her younger sibling was voicing or acting out a scene from a movie. According to Sarah, Laura would sit upright in bed, eyes fixed on the doorway, and tell an invisible someone to leave them alone. Whenever Sarah asked for details in the morning, Laura would pretend she couldn't remember.

Her sister had been the first person to describe Laura as gifted. For knowing stuff no one else did. At four years old, Laura had told her parents and sister how much she enjoyed playing with her blond, blue-eyed big brother in her dreams. Only in the last two years had they learned about their mother's loss – a boy – late in her first pregnancy.

***

The next morning, with the news report from the previous night playing over in her mind, Laura borrowed Sarah's beloved 2001 Holden Barina and drove to Joanna's. She told her mother she was going to the shops to pick up a few things. Sarah handed her the keys with a knowing look. Yogi rode shotgun.

The Thompson property was on a small acreage at the edge of town, and was unlike other homes or properties in the area. The front yard was a riot of colour and noise – vibrant red bottle brush, soft pink grevilleas, and bright yellow wattle were dotted in no real order across the lawn, and a large tea tree stood beside the front verandah. Unlike the garden at her house, there were no neat hedges, English roses, or towering oak trees. Mr Thompson loved native plants, and everything he cared for belonged and thrived – was part of the natural environment. Squawking lorikeets flew between the shrubs, chewing on flowers or hanging upside down like crazy acrobats. Each year, they raised their babies in the tea tree next to the house. Laura loved their boisterous, funny antics.

Laura liked every member of the Thompson family, and even though they were younger than her, she'd had a crush on

Benny and Jordy since she was old enough to know what a crush felt like. Not that she told a soul; others in town had strong opinions about the Thompson clan. Laura knew the family was not treated the same as everyone else. Joanna was only a toddler when her mother died, and all her life she'd lived with whispers and rumours about her father. Laura knew Mr Thompson; she'd seen how much he loved his children. He was a gentle but reserved man, withdrawn, and wary of strangers. Laura didn't believe he'd hurt anyone and chose to go by her dad's advice: the number one rule in life was to treat other people the way you wanted to be treated. Laura knew her mother didn't approve of Joanna's reckless behaviour, and she'd hidden the training sessions for so long, to avoid upsetting her father, that secrecy had become a habit.

The Thompsons accepted her the way she was. They didn't judge Laura because she liked to play footy and hang out with her dog and didn't have a lot of friends or a cute boyfriend, and they never commented on her poor fashion sense. In turn, she refused to listen to small-town gossip.

The emotions she'd tried to keep under control over the last twenty-four hours threatened to spill over as she stopped the car at the entrance to the drive. Getting out to open the gate, she stared at the weatherboard house, and it hit her. Never again would she run with Benny and Jordy. Never again would they challenge her and Joanna. Never again would they tease her. She wanted to cry, but if she gave in to her feelings, if she let the tears fall, she wasn't sure they'd ever stop. She swallowed her grief and stepped back into the car. She didn't want to upset Joanna.

The two girls had become close friends and fierce competitors from their first day at primary school, racing each other every day on the oval at lunchtime. Benny and Jordy had also been excellent sprinters, but in the last couple of years, they'd focused on rugby league. They were stars of the district footy side – the Wallabies – bookending the team as wingers and lighting up the game with their speed and ball-handling skills. People talked about them having the talent to break into the New South Wales Rugby League first-grade competition. Others said they had the skills to be as good as players like legendary Eels winger Eric Grothe, or to rival current-day players like Jordan Rapana, Selwyn Cobbo, or Josh Addo-Carr. High praise and well-deserved, thought Laura, who'd seen them play.

Football also ran in Laura's blood; Jack and Henry were both talented rugby league players in their youth, and Laura followed in their footsteps. Jeannie, who was frightened that her petite daughter could be seriously injured, had stopped Laura from playing competition.

So, Laura channelled her energy into sprinting, using the homemade racing lanes Arthur Thompson had carved out in his back paddock for his kids. Whenever Arthur wasn't working, he coached them and chastised Benny and Jordy when they taunted

Laura about her short legs. Little did anyone know the teasing only spurred Laura on.

As she gripped the steering wheel, she thought about the one person who needed her the most, Joanna. Chugging up the Thompsons' driveway, Laura saw her friend sitting on the edge of the front verandah, forced a smile and waved out the window.

Joanna met her partway down the drive, pointing to a spot near the tea tree. 'Park over there. Dad's not good. He had a bad night, and, well, it's not a good time for you to be here right now. My aunties and uncles are arriving soon.' Joanna glanced back at the house, motioning for Laura and Yogi to follow her across the yard to a large gum tree. As they passed the Thompsons' car, Laura noticed pieces of glass on the bonnet and a hole in the windscreen.

Leaning against the trunk and sitting in the shade, hidden from the view of the house, Laura pushed away memories of happy times with Joanna, Benny, and Jordy – gulping down soft drinks, teasing each other, and trading footy cards. She went to ask the question that was burning her up inside. 'Your brothers-'

'Don't!' Joanna interrupted. Then, lowering her voice so Laura had to lean closer to hear her, she said, 'They took off a couple of days ago, which they do sometimes. Normally, they grab a ride to visit family in Sydney, but no one had seen or heard from them. We were all out searching, but no one thought they would be in the gorge. Not near the bridge. No one was searching there.'

Tears rolled down Joanna's cheeks, and Laura took her friend's hand, squeezing it tight.

'Dad's so angry,' Joanna said, staring at Laura, her chocolate-brown eyes blazing. 'He thinks the coppers didn't treat it seriously. They brushed him off. Told him my brothers had 'most likely taken off'. Said they have a history of skipping school and disappearing for a few days, so Dad called Uncle Leo.' Uncle Leo was Leo Thompson – a well-known and respected senator for New South Wales in the federal parliament. 'He can push the police to do a proper investigation. No way were they playing around on the bridge and fell.'

'It's good the police are looking into it,' Laura said, her voice trailing off as she realised how lame she sounded.

Joanna thumped the ground. 'My brothers know *not* to hang out there. We stay away from that place.'

'Because of your mum?' Laura whispered. She and Joanna never talked about Kathleen Thompson. Joanna had never wanted to discuss her mother.

'Yeah, I mean, Dad always thought the gorge was haunted. But now he's convinced it's cursed. You've heard the stories. People say they've seen a man holding a baby in his arms by the trees near the cliff or down by the waterhole. When they try to talk to him, he disappears. Other people have heard a baby crying, but there's no one there.'

Laura felt the air being squeezed out of her lungs. 'I've heard the stories too,' she breathed.

Joanna continued. 'Terrible things have happened at the gorge. That place is rotten, and this town is … It's bad country.'

'Bad? But …' Laura faltered. She wanted to disagree. To her, the gorge was special. A place she felt at peace. At times, she reckoned it called to her. 'Surely your dad doesn't *really* believe it's cursed?'

'Dad says our family is tied to this place, by blood. My brothers knew how Dad felt about the gorge; that's why they wouldn't hang out there.'

They sat, not speaking, each girl lost in her thoughts until a magpie landed in the tree above them, its song breaking the silence. 'My dad told me that in the old tales, a single magpie is considered unlucky and three together mean someone in your family will die. I saw three magpies in this same tree the day my brothers went missing,' Joanna said as the magpie stared at them.

'But you've never believed in the old stories before.'

'Yeah, well, maybe I need to start,' Joanna said as the magpie flew off.

Laura fingered the tattered footy card in her back pocket, her mind straying back to her dreams.

She was torn. Part of her wanted to share with Joanna what she'd dreamt. She wanted to tell her that she thought someone had hurt Benny and Jordy. The other part of her – the part that had spent her adolescence suppressing her thoughts and feelings – won the battle. Now was not the time to discuss her dreams, or her feelings. Joanna had lost her little brothers. Her anger and grief were raw. She didn't want to upset her friend further and was worried Joanna might think she was making stuff up or, worse still, decide Laura was nuts. Laura could still hear the cries of 'Loopy Laura' echoing through the playground.

Sometimes, in her dreams, she was the one in danger, like when she sensed the unsettling presence of the Shadow Man or had her falling dream. But most of the time, Laura's dreams were of other people, and even as a small child she'd had the gift of second sight – and been in trouble for telling people about it.

Like what had happened with Stephen, a boy in her kindergarten class. Stephen was always in trouble at school. Every week, he spent time in the naughty corner. One night, Laura dreamt of Stephen. He was leaning over in the corner at the front of the class, his hands on top of his head as usual, snickering at the teacher who'd had enough of his cheek. Snickering turned to screams, and Laura saw him cowering under a kitchen table while his father beat his mother. The image shifted, and she saw Stephen shielding himself and his younger brother as blows rained down on them.

The next day they were playing tag when Laura caught Stephen, and before letting him go, she murmured, 'Your dad. He hurts you and your mum and –'

'Don't be stupid,' Stephen hissed, slapping her hand away, and at that moment, he became the self-appointed head of the 'Loopy Laura' fan club.

Luckily for Laura, she'd had Joanna and her brothers. No, she corrected herself. She *used to* have Benny and Jordy.

***

After leaving the Thompson property, Laura went to the corner store to buy Sarah a magazine and some chocolate for herself. Sarah had worked every weekend and holiday at the orchard for the last four years, picking fruit to pay for her car and support her university studies, and she'd given Laura a few dollars on the pretext of getting out of the house. Laura would miss her sister. She looked out for her – understood her.

Driving home, Laura couldn't stop thinking about what Joanna had said about the gorge being cursed and that she thought it was bad country. She'd wanted to stay longer, to comfort Joanna, but understood they were grieving and Mr Thompson wanted privacy. Joanna had confided to Laura that her father had been interviewed by the police about her brothers. Told Laura they'd even had a rock thrown through the windscreen of their car. Arthur had torn up the note that was tied to the rock before Joanna could read what it said and Joanna let loose some choice swear words about the stupidity of small-town minds.

But all Laura could think about was Benny and Jordy. She couldn't stop picturing their bodies lying motionless on the rocks. She'd only seen one dead person in her life. Great-grandmother Bridget had passed on when Laura was seven; the entire family had held hands and prayed as she slipped away. Before the funeral, they'd held a viewing, with an open coffin allowing mourners to say a final goodbye. There she was, Bridget Malone, dressed in her Sunday best, hands folded on her chest, her cheek cold under Laura's kiss.

Laura had loved her feisty great-grandmother's funny Irish brogue, sharp wit, and acid tongue, but in the months after her death, she'd experienced a disturbing, recurring dream in which Bridget Malone took the place of Saint Patrick in a picture hanging in Gran's bedroom. In the painting, Bridget was not standing on the beach in Ireland. Instead, she was at the edge of a cliff, holding her crucifix in one hand, arms extended, eyes wide. The elderly woman called a warning Laura couldn't hear. After the dream, whenever Laura walked past Gran's room, she swore the eyes of Saint Patrick followed her. She had not thought about the death of her great-grandmother or the painting dream for a long time.

Chapter 9 – The gorge

Barefoot and shivering in only a thin nightdress, Laura dares poke her head around the trunk of the tree. At the same time, the early morning chortle of a kookaburra on a branch above heralds the start of a new day.

An eerie silence follows, and every muscle in Laura's body tenses.

Has he seen her?

A man with dirty-blond hair shoves a skinny, red-haired man in the back with a long rifle, pushing him towards the edge of a cliff. 'Move it,' he growls.

As the ginger-haired man stumbles to the ground, a baby cries.

'Shut that child up,' the blond man shouts.

On his knees, the red-haired man turns, and Laura realises he's not much older than her. He holds a newborn in the air as he pleads for its life, his words tumbling out. 'Please, I beg ye, show some mercy. If not for me, then for the babe.'

Lowering the old-fashioned rifle to the sobbing man's head, the blond man says, 'I'll show you mercy. I'll give you a choice. Jump or be shot.'

Silencing a gasp with one hand to her mouth while gathering the flyaway nightgown with the other, Laura creeps closer.

'Stop,' a man pants, crashing his way through the scrub into the clearing by the cliff. Hands out, he tries to reason with the enraged man. 'Jeremiah, don't do this. Think about it. You'll be hung or sent to Norfolk. You have a baby to think of – an heir.'

Jeremiah grabs the cowering man by the collar as he swings the firearm towards the newcomer. 'An heir,' he scoffs. 'That's no child of mine. Look at it. Ginger hair like its filthy Irish father. If you'd disciplined this one like I told you, Thompson, then he would never have dared to consort with my wife. There's only one place for adulterers and bastards. Hell.'

Thompson charges at Jeremiah, trying to knock the gun from his hand. As they struggle, the younger man tries to break free, but Jeremiah holds on to him, hurling the desperate man, and the baby in his arms, over the edge. Screams and the sound of crashing rocks fill the air.

The two men continue fighting before Jeremiah rams the butt of the rifle into the side of the other man's head. Thompson falls to the ground, unconscious.

Laura has to help the brave, defenceless man.

With that thought fuelling her courage, Laura steps out from behind the cover of her tree.

'Stop!' she calls, but her voice is lost among the echo of more screams.

***

Laura wakes, sweat covering her nightie. Thompson! The man who tried to stop Jeremiah must be related to Joanna.

Sneaking a peek at Sarah, she can see she hasn't stirred.

Thank God! She wouldn't have to explain the dream to her sister.

Chapter 10 – Laura

February 2020

One month after finding Benny and Jordy Thompson at the bottom of the gorge, locals were still coming to grips with the tragedy. The autopsy report said there were no traces of alcohol or drugs. While the report was inconclusive, the coroner said it was unlikely the boys had fallen or even jumped to their deaths from the bridge; the type of injuries and the position of the bodies indicated the boys may have been victims of foul play.

Since the death of Benny and Jordy, tensions in the town had reached boiling point. Without a prime suspect, some outspoken locals continued to speculate that Arthur Thompson had something to do with the death of his sons, and the grieving father retreated further from everyday life in Wallaby Rock. Media outlets lost interest in the case, despite ongoing agitation from Senator Thompson, who pleaded for more investigative resources to be deployed.

Laura was struggling with school. When she wasn't dreaming of Benny and Jordy being stalked, she was haunted by her falling dream and the disturbing presence of the Shadow Man. Then there was Liv Hansen to deal with. She kept posting nasty videos of Laura and spreading them through the school. But the worst of it all was the guilt Laura felt in keeping her connection to the Thompsons a secret from her family.

The only things keeping her going were her favourite subjects, physical education and history. A new headmistress for sport had started the school's first athletics squad, and Laura made the team, but it was difficult to attend training sessions after school. Doing so meant she would miss the bus and her family would have to make the long trek to school to collect her. Laura knew the farm came first, and the journey to pick her up was time out her family couldn't afford. In the end, she trained only one day a week with the squad, but her father repeated his promise to help her train at home. It was Laura's last chance to make the state team, the last opportunity to prove she had what it took to be one of the best in the country.

Laura hadn't seen much of Joanna. She was too busy trying to keep up with her studies and help with the milking and other farm chores.

***

When Laura couldn't take another moment chained to her desk with her head buried in her laptop she begged Sarah, who was home for the weekend, to drop her at Joanna's while she caught up with friends at the pub. She missed Joanna and wanted to check on her and talk about stuff like they used to do. Laura was excited to share her news about joining the athletics squad and to confide in her about the dream of the man at the gorge.

Sarah left Laura and Yogi at the gate, telling her sister she'd pick her up on the way home. But as the pair approached the Thompsons' house, Laura realised something wasn't right. Joanna's father took pride in his home and loved his garden. Laura often saw him mowing the lawn and trimming the trees. No one was on the verandah, and with the windows closed and the curtains drawn, the house appeared empty. The family car was parked at the top of the drive, but grass and weeds had grown around the tyres. Laura was about to turn around and start the long walk into town when the front door creaked open.

Joanna's father stood in the doorway, shielding his eyes against the sun. 'Who is it?'

'Mr Thompson, it's me, Laura. Is Joanna home?'

Within seconds of Mr Thompson calling his daughter, Joanna appeared in the doorway, and the two girls stared at each other until Laura pointed to the verandah.

Joanna looked tired. Her clothes were dirty; her hair was a tangled mess. Joanna always moved with energy and purpose, but today, she appeared listless. Not even Yogi's wagging tail got a response.

They perched on the edge of wooden boards, Laura kicking at the overgrown lawn.

'You haven't been around,' Joanna began.

'I know. I'm sorry. I've been busy with school and the farm,' Laura replied, realising how pathetic she sounded.

'Too busy on weekends?' Joanna asked.

'How are you?' Laura asked, hoping to change the subject.

'Fine. Can't you tell? We're all fine.' Joanna's voice oozed sarcasm.

'Joanna, about your brothers …'

'Don't,' said Joanna, her voice cracking. 'We don't talk about them. Dad's taken their photos down and refuses to speak their names or even mention them. It's like he doesn't want to remember. Poor Dad … He … He isn't the same. And as for those bloody useless coppers …' Joanna's anger erupted. 'The mongrels wouldn't know if their bums were on fire. I bet if it was someone else's kids, they'd still be investigating. But the Thompsons? Nah, they don't care about us. The police suck.'

Laura knew what people thought of Joanna and her father and had seen firsthand how they were treated.

***

Last summer, Laura and Joanna had met at the shop. They'd taken their time perusing ice cream flavours and flicking through magazines, arguing whether Chris Hemsworth was cuter than Zac Efron. It was a conversation they'd had many times before. Laura was team Zac but Joanna was Thor all the way. 'Laura, it's no contest. Come on. Just look at those biceps … and those abs,' Joanna insisted as she waved a photo of a buff Chris Hemsworth working out on the beach in front of her friend. 'Zac is cute, sure, but he's no Thor.'

Their close inspection of the Hollywood stars was interrupted by the shopkeeper, Mrs Bagnall. Mrs Old Bag, as she'd been nicknamed, pulled Joanna aside roughly, poked a finger in her face, and yelled, 'Are you going to buy something or not? I'm sick of you coming in here, sneaking around. I've had enough. Bugger off. Go on, get!'

After recovering from the shock of Mrs Old Bag's spray, Laura had spoken up in defence of her friend and been told she could get out too.

Laura had avoided the shop for as long as she could, and whenever she entered the store, Mrs Old Bag refused to speak to her unless necessary. It had taken ages to convince Joanna to return.

'The police don't suck,' Laura said, gazing across the long grass. 'Everyone liked your brothers, Joanna. You know I did.' Laura hesitated before continuing. 'I need to ask you about something. I had a dream – after you told me about the gorge. Has your dad told you anything more about what happened back then?'

Joanna watched colour flood Laura's cheeks, a telltale sign of nerves. 'Why? What did you dream?'

'I was hiding behind a tree. There was a man, and he had an old-looking rifle pointed at a young man and a baby on a cliff.

He was shouting at the man to jump or be shot. Then another man arrived. He tried to save them, but he couldn't. Screaming woke me up. I think the man who tried to help may have been related to you.'

Joanna's eyes widened. 'You saw it,' she said, edging away. 'Dad and Uncle Leo told me the full story a couple of weeks after the funeral. They said our ancestor, George Thompson, an ex-convict, was granted a large slice of land here. He had a neighbour, Jeremiah Pyke, who was also an ex-convict, but they didn't get along. They fought over land and water from the river. One night, Jeremiah dragged one of George's convicts to a cliff, forcing the man to take his newborn child along with him, and then pushed them both over the edge. That's why everyone thinks the gorge is haunted. My dad thinks it's the ghost of the convict man and baby that people see and hear.'

'What happened to Jeremiah and to your ancestor, to George?'

'Jeremiah escaped and was never seen again and probably died in the bush. George survived, but we only have a few acres of the old property left. That's where Dad and I live, on the edge of what was the original Thompson farm. Over the years, our family has had a lot of bad luck and the land was sold off piece by piece. But there's always been a Thompson at Wallaby Rock.'

Laura had no idea what to say. She'd heard the stories but never quite believed them. Then came her dream. Why was she seeing this? What did it mean? Was this the reason the gorge called her?

'You stay away from there, Laura,' Joanna warned, her voice sharp. Her friend's harsh tone made Laura jump, and she realised she'd drifted off into her thoughts – 'disconnecting', Sarah had labelled it, when Laura went quiet for too long during a conversation. 'You see and feel too much. It's not good for you to be there,' Joanna said.

As she gazed into her friend's eyes, Laura had the odd sensation she was falling again. This time into a deep well of sadness.

'Joanna, would you like to come over for tea?' Laura was worried about her friend and was sure her mother would welcome Joanna to their home, considering all she'd been through.

'No, I need to be here – keep an eye on Dad, you know, but thanks.'

Standing up, Laura got ready to leave. 'I'd better get going. Catch you soon?'

'Sure,' Joanna replied.

Chapter 11 – Laura

Laura made more of an effort to stay in touch with Joanna, but their friendship was different. Joanna's reaction to Laura's dream had reinforced in her mind that it was best not to share her dreams or feelings with anyone. She didn't want anything to get in the way of the bond her and Joanna shared.

Joanna was also preoccupied. She'd started dating a man from the footy club, a mate of her brothers who was ten years older. The relationship had tongues wagging all over town.

But as hard as she tried, Laura couldn't get the story Joanna had shared about the killing at the gorge out of her head. One evening, she asked Gran if she'd ever heard of the Pykes and if Jeremiah was behind the death of a convict man and baby at the cliff. Laura wanted to know if Grace thought this was the source of the legend about the gorge being haunted.

'Where did you hear that?' Grace snapped as her knitting needles clicked up and down.

'I heard some kids talking the other day,' Laura said.

'Well, there were lots of disputes in the early days – that's true. Between settlers and between farmers and the local Aboriginal people.' Grace put the half-finished scarf to one side. 'If you're so interested, I could ask permission for you to read some of the society's records.'

Grace was a member of the Wallaby Rock Historical Society, which met every month at the town hall.

Laura's eyes lit up. 'Yes, please.'

****

That Saturday, Grace told Laura she could join her to examine the society's records, but not before first reinforcing the importance of treating the artifacts with care and respect.

Grace and the president of the society, Eileen Godwin, were in the small kitchen at the back of the hall making a fresh pot of tea while Laura sat at a table scattered with old books and copies of papers. Pulling on gloves, Laura opened a leather-bound book. It was the diary of a woman named Anne Kelly – the wife of Benjamin Kelly, who built Wallaby Rock's original pub, The Royal Mail. The first entry was dated 2 August 1821.

After much hard labour, the inn opened last month. My good husband, Benjamin, and our sons William and Harold have toiled for many a day, and I am proud to say word has spread as far as Sydney town about the quality of our ale, the warmth of our hearth, and the heartiness of our stew. God willing, we will be blessed with good custom.

Business is slow, but as more upstanding families settle in the district, I pray things will improve. To date, our lodging has been most welcomed by weary travellers taking the long road to settlements further south.

Laura skimmed the next few pages, which detailed the challenges the Kelly family faced in getting barley for their ale. Now and then, Laura recognised the surname of a family who was living in the area. Anne Kelly's diary entry dated 10 October 1821 caught her attention.

Today I met a most agreeable gentleman, Frederick Murray. Mr Murray and his wife, Maureen, who is heavy with child, have been granted land by the Governor and intend to set up a small dairy farm in the area. Mr Murray received a pardon and grant of land from the Governor and confessed he had been sentenced for not only the theft of a pig but for making and selling bacon. Benjamin disappeared for a short while, later showing me where he'd hidden our valuables!

Mr Murray hails from county Galway, and in conversing with him, my heart started to ache for the old country. Leaving Ireland for a new life in New South Wales was a difficult decision but one Benjamin and I hope will provide a brighter future for our children. My spirit longs for the rolling green hills and soft rain of home, but we are committed to making our new life as free settlers in the colonies a success.

Laura was excited to read about her ancestors and ran into the kitchen to share the diary entry with Grace, who grinned and said they must make a copy. Laura kept flicking through the diary in which Anne Kelly sporadically recorded the events of her family and the expanding district. An entry dated 3 May 1822 read:

News about fighting between the Thompsons and Pykes worries all of us. Last night, Jeremiah Pyke claimed he lost twenty head of sheep because he couldn't get enough water for his stock. He blamed George Thompson, claiming his neighbour was taking more than his fair share from the river. Jeremiah had a head of steam and talked in a blustering manner about taking matters into his own hands. Benjamin cut off his ale and put him to bed to sleep off his languor. I fear a dark cloud hangs over Mr Pyke.

Laura skimmed the rest of Anne Kelly's diary and reviewed a collection of other journals and papers. She was starting to think she would not find anything else when the name Pyke caught her eye. She pulled a paper towards her. It was a copy of a letter from Jeremiah Pyke to the Governor of New South Wales, dated 27 June 1822.

Major-General Sir Thomas Brisbane
Governor of New South Wales

Your excellency,

I write to you seeking aid for the good people of the district of Wallaby Rock. In his wisdom and generosity, his excellency Governor Macquarie granted me thirty acres of land, and I have toiled night and day to make good for our growing colony.

My efforts, however, are hampered by the unconscionable conduct of my neighbour, George Thompson.

As he has a larger land holding, Mr Thompson believes he can take as much water as he deems fit from the river, leaving little for my sheep and crops. I have lost many animals due to the dry climate and lack of water. This must be addressed.

Furthermore, Mr Thompson has male and female convicts in his care but does not discipline them, giving these wretched creatures a view of their station that is beyond their standing.

I believe the establishment of a regiment in the district to enforce the law is warranted. Indeed, I consider it critical to the future prosperity of New South Wales, and I implore you to send forth men to survey the situation.

I am pleased to report our inn can accommodate up to ten men, and the food and ale are good fare. Your men would be looked after.

I await your reply.

Your humble servant as always,

Jeremiah Pyke

Laura read and re-read the letter. As far as she knew, no Pykes were living in Wallaby Rock, and she wondered what happened to them. She also wondered if the governor had sent troops to the district as Jeremiah Pyke had requested. Laura questioned Grace about the Pykes, but it was Mrs Godwin, a walking Wikipedia on everything to do with early settlement in Wallaby Rock, who answered. 'Pykes? Oh yes, they settled here, but no Pykes live here now. There are some Pykes buried in the old cemetery, though,' Mrs Godwin said as she made a copy of the letter for Laura.

After going through the rest of the records, Laura couldn't find any official reports naming Jeremiah as the one responsible for the death of the convict and baby. She did, however, have evidence of the feud between the two families.

As Laura helped Gran and Mrs Godwin pack away the records, she asked if there might be any other papers or journals.

'Most of our original records are kept in the State Library in Sydney. We keep a few original items here, along with copies of the most important records held in Sydney,' Mrs Godwin told her.

'Oh, I see,' said Laura. 'Can anyone read the State Library records?'

'Of course, but you need to know what you're searching for. I take it you weren't successful?'

'Not exactly, but thank you for letting me try,' Laura said.

Mrs Godwin smiled. 'You are most welcome, Laura. I wish more young people took an interest in their local history.'

Chapter 12 – Laura

On a Friday afternoon at the beginning of March, Laura's world was turned upside down again.

She was sitting at the front of the school bus, chatting to the driver, George. Hers was one of the last stops, and the bus was almost empty. George had the radio on in the background and turned it up when a newsflash came on saying a body had been discovered in bushland. The two of them listened in.

'In breaking news, police today revealed the body of a woman in her early twenties has been discovered in bushland near Wallaby Rock. The death is the third in the district this year and follows the unexplained death of twin teenagers – Benny and Jordy Thompson – in January. Police say it is early days in the investigation, but they are treating this latest death as suspicious.'

The news that yet another body had been found in Wallaby Rock was everywhere – #bodyinthebush was trending on social media and it was the headline story on Jacquie's blog, *Tales from the Rock*.

On the evening news, John Gordon, who had covered the story about Benny and Jordy, also reported on the latest tragedy. Standing in front of a long row of cherry trees, Gordon swatted flies away as he spoke to the camera.

'The body has been identified as Yvette Berger, a 23-year-old German woman on a working visa who had been picking cherries in this orchard, located thirty kilometres south of Wallaby Rock. Ms Berger's vehicle was found burnt out on a secluded back road by orchard owner Mr Tony Sias, who notified police. Ms Berger is one of many European backpackers who pick fruit each year to fund their travels around Australia. We understand Ms Berger was preparing to return home in a week. A trip and family reunion that will now, sadly, never happen.'

Pictures of people picking crops appeared on screen, the footage shifting to images of thick bushland, the bridge, the gorge, and Wallaby Rock's main street.

'Police say they are treating this as a murder investigation. A young couple discovered Ms Berger while bushwalking through the local gorge, three kilometres from where twin teenage boys were found dead earlier this year. Police investigating the murder of Ms Berger say, at this stage, they have no evidence connecting this case to the deaths of Benny and Jordy Thompson. We understand Ms Berger's parents are on their way to Australia to take their daughter home.'

The camera returned to Mr Gordon, who wrapped up his report.

'This is John Gordon reporting.'

The gorge. Again? Laura stared, fixated on the screen, tomato sauce dripping onto her hand from the sausage that hung suspended in mid-air by her fork. She watched as the thick liquid oozed down her arm, and an image of the boys forced its way into her mind – blood pooling around their skulls. She bit into the meat and almost gagged.

***

That night, Bridget Malone once more visited Laura in her dreams. Her great-grandmother was more agitated than before. Bridget kept calling out, but as hard as Laura tried to listen, she couldn't hear her. The world tipped sideways, and she was falling again, spiralling downward. Trapped on her bed, Laura was surrounded by terrified faces while screams and the wail of a baby crying filled her ears.

Awake, fear still gripped Laura, and the hairs on her arms stood like sentinels as she turned to face the doorway. A dark figure was staring back. *Shadow Man!* Unable to scream, Laura rubbed her eyes, and when she opened them again, he was gone.

***

By morning, Laura had decided she needed answers. On her way to the kitchen, she saw her mother sewing in a chair in the sitting room, next to the piano. It was her mother's favourite spot to sit and listen to Sarah practise.

In the kitchen, Grace was packing away dishes.

'You're up late this morning,' Grace commented, and Laura felt Gran's eyes boring into the back of her head.

'I had a restless night.'

'I'll leave the water in so you can wash up once you've had some breakfast. You must be hungry,' Grace said as she wiped the palms of her hands on her apron.

'Thanks, Gran.' Laura paused before ploughing on. 'Gran, do you remember Mrs Godwin saying there may be more records from early settlement in the State Library?'

'Yes, but what are you trying to find?' Grace pierced Laura with a knowing look.

'I thought I might be able to find evidence of the feud between the Pykes and Thompsons. Verify the old legends. I spoke to my history teacher, Mr Herbert, and he said I could research this for my final history assignment. We've been studying Australian history,' Laura explained.

'You'd better speak to your parents. I know your mother wouldn't want you going to Sydney on your own.' Grace waved her hand in the air when Laura rolled her eyes. 'I know. I know. You're eighteen now, an adult. But your mother still worries about you. You'll understand one day if you have children of your own. How about I go with you? We can take the train in and visit Sarah while we're there.'

Laura hugged her grandmother. They all missed Sarah, but no one more than Laura.

'Thanks, Gran.' Laura ran to the sitting room and explained to her mum how visiting the library would help her get a good mark on her history assignment and they could also check in on Sarah.

***

The following weekend, Laura and Grace boarded the Country Express bound for Central at 6.30 am. They changed trains partway through, swapping from the country to the city line. Laura read while Grace caught up on her knitting. After they got off at Central, they walked several blocks to the library, and Laura's neck was sore from watching the people around her. Even though it was a Saturday, everyone was in a tearing hurry, and no one smiled or talked to each other. Very different to life in Wallaby Rock.

Laura had never been to the State Library, and as they approached the large steps in front of the building, she stopped, goggling at the imposing statue of Matthew Flinders, who stood like a guardian near the entrance.

Once inside, Grace, in her most refined voice, asked a dour and bored-looking woman how they might find records of white settlement. They were directed to the computer room, where they could search for and order books or records to read. Grace let slip her membership of the Wallaby Rock Historical Society, and the woman sat up, smiled, and offered to show them where to go and how to access the files.

As they followed their new friend, Grace leaned down and whispered to Laura, 'Remember, darling, you catch more flies with honey.'

They had been reading journals and copies of letters for over an hour when Laura discovered a letter from Governor Brisbane to Jeremiah Pyke of Pyke Farm, dated 3 September 1822.

Dear Mr Pyke,

I thank you for your correspondence and for bringing to my attention the situation in the Wallaby Rock district.

While I understand your frustration at the loss of stock and supplies, the rule of law must be upheld. Any disputes should be brought to my attention and addressed through proper channels. If you wish to pursue this matter, you must bring your case to Sydney for due consideration.

As we reach inland to explore new lands and opportunities for our colony and try to keep peace with the natives, it is more important than ever for us all to work together to avoid any unnecessary confrontation.

Yours in good faith,

Major General Sir Thomas Brisbane

His Excellency, the Governor of New South Wales

Laura was excited and showed the letter to Grace before rushing off to make a copy. It proved the governor at the time had not supported Jeremiah Pyke's request to take immediate action. What it didn't prove, however, was whether Jeremiah had taken matters into his own hands.

Grace suggested they research the Pykes in the hope of coming across letters or other information referring to the incident at the gorge. They knew Pykes no longer lived in Wallaby Rock, but why had they left, and where had they gone?

By searching convict records, they found that Jeremiah had lived in London and had been sentenced to seven years for fraud. He was transported to the colonies, where he was pardoned after serving only five years due to his diligent work on government farms in Parramatta. Ironically, he'd been appointed as head bookkeeper. He was granted thirty acres in the Wallaby Rock district and settled there with his wife, Margaret.

As hard as they tried, Laura and Grace could not find anything else about the Pykes or whether Jeremiah had acted without the governor's consent.

At midday, on the steps of the library, they met Sarah, who led them to a nearby pub. Sitting in a shady beer garden, they enjoyed steak sandwiches and chips. Grace indulged in a shandy – a half beer/half lemonade – and Laura sucked down a schooner of ale while Sarah, who was sporting a new pink hairdo, ordered red wine. Laura raised her eyebrows and stuck out her little finger at her sister. 'Getting fancy now, aren't you, Sis?'

Sarah laughed and poked her in the arm. Laura wanted to spend the rest of the day with her sister, but time was running out; they needed to get back to the library and on the last train home at 4.30 pm.

After two more hours searching library records, Grace stumbled across journal extracts from the explorations of Lieutenant John Oxley.

On the 30th day of November 1822, accompanied by two of my men and my guide, Jimmy, I journeyed to Wallaby Rock to explore the area and report back to the Governor on the state of agricultural production. The Governor further requested I investigate a dispute between two families.

I met with Jeremiah Pyke, who claimed his neighbour, George Thompson, was taking more than he was entitled to from the nearby river. He also claimed Mr Thompson did not discipline his convicts, alleging this could lead to further crimes and insurrection as the convicts in question became bolder.

Mistress Pyke, a shy young woman, fled when she saw me and my men, refusing to speak to us. When I inquired about this behaviour, her husband said his wife had experienced rough treatment at the hands of officers in the past.

That night, while camped at the river, our guide, Jimmy, found a nearby tribe who spoke to him of attacks by white men and said they now lived in fear. When asked what these men looked like, they described a man resembling Mr Pyke.

I returned to Pyke Farm on our journey home to discuss the matter. Jeremiah Pyke refused to elaborate and ordered us to leave. At the stables, we were met by his wife who was heavy with child. Her face was bruised and swollen. She wept and begged me to take her away from her husband. She told us he took pleasure in punishing his men and attacking the natives. Mistress Pyke said her husband was a jealous and violent man intent on bringing down his neighbour.

I will report these matters to Governor Brisbane on my return. While it is not the Crown's role to interfere in the sanctity of marriage, I pitied the poor soul.

Laura stared open-mouthed at Gran. At last!

Chapter 13 – Laura

April 2020

Between trying to transition to online schooling with patchy internet, training, and chores, Laura had no time to dwell on what they'd uncovered at the library.

While working on her history assignment, she found other occurrences of disputes or feuds between farmers and more reports of fighting and even massacres of Australia's Aboriginal people. When Aboriginal people were mentioned in historical texts, they were often painted as agitators and a barrier to growth and expansion. Laura was shocked to discover it was only in 1971 that Aboriginal and Torres Strait Islander people were included in the census, a regular survey of the nation's population.

Laura kept returning to her notes about the feud between George Thompson and Jeremiah Pyke. She wanted to help Joanna, and her father, to shift people's views of the family. One way of doing that was to prove their ancestor was a good person, to tell people it was George Thompson who tried to help the man and baby. That it was George who'd tried to save their lives, and it was Jeremiah Pyke who was responsible for their deaths – deaths that Laura believed were the source of the local myths and ghost stories. If George was a good man, who tried to save others, then maybe people in town would think better of the Thompsons today. And maybe, just maybe, by shedding light on what happened all those years ago, Laura could change people's perceptions of the gorge and show how beautiful and peaceful it was.

There had to be a way to help, even if only in a small way. It was her history teacher, Mr Herbert, who gave her the answer.

During one of her online history lessons during lockdown, Laura shared with Mr Herbert what she'd uncovered about the deaths at the gorge in 1822 and what Joanna had told her. The enthusiastic history teacher commended her on her initiative and said a friend at Sydney University might be interested in the information. Mr Herbert said his friend might be able to get the story published and placed on official records for the first time. While Laura had spent her life shying away from attention and staying out of trouble wherever possible, she wanted this, for Joanna and her father.

But first, she needed to talk to Mr Thompson about John Oxley's suspicions of Jeremiah Pyke.

Laura had planned to catch up with Joanna and Mr Thompson at the inter-district athletics carnival scheduled for June, but all excursions and carnivals had been shelved due to COVID. Laura kept training at home. It wasn't a great set-up. Nothing like Joanna's homemade racing lanes, but it would do for now. Laura kept hoping she would have a chance to prove herself against the best in the state one last time.

While everyone was out, Laura video-called Joanna on her phone. The connection kept buffering, but it was the best she could do for now.

The Joanna who appeared onscreen seemed to be more herself, not as tired or sad. 'Hey, Joanna. How're you going?' Laura asked.

'Hi, Laura. I'm okay. What's up?'

'How's your dad? Is he any better?'

'A little,' Joanna said, lowering her voice. 'In a way, lockdown has helped. It's given him an excuse to work from home and avoid other people.'

'That's good,' Laura said. 'Hey, do you reckon I could speak to him about the story you told me? I've been searching for records of it. I even visited the State Library in Sydney a few weeks ago. I found something, but I'd like to check it with him.'

'Don't you believe me?' Joanna snapped.

'Yeah, I do. Honestly. But I want to understand it better. I want to make it official. Clear your family's name. Show everyone the Thompsons are good people.'

'You think finding evidence of what happened at the gorge two hundred years ago will make people think *my* family, *my* dad, or *me*, are decent people? Good luck,' Joanna scoffed.

'Look, I know it might sound silly, but I think this could help your dad … and you. Have you heard about the German woman? Everything keeps pointing to the gorge. To our town. You said yourself it's … bad country.'

'I'll speak to Dad,' Joanna said. 'He might talk to you.'

'Thanks. I can talk over the phone or video or even sneak over to your place. Let me know what he says.'

'Sure. See you soon,' Joanna said.

'Yeah, see ya,' Laura replied as she ended the call.

A few days later, Laura got a text message from Joanna saying her father would talk to her but would prefer to do it face-to-face.

On Saturday morning, Laura stayed in her room, pretending to study, waiting for Grace and Jeannie to go shopping. She didn't want to tell them where she was going.

Jack and Henry had taken the ute to help a neighbour repair fences, and Laura seized the chance to pull out the family's ageing dirt bike and visit Joanna. If her parents found out she'd taken the small motorbike out, especially when everyone was meant to be avoiding contact with each other, she'd cop it big time. Yogi ran beside her as she approached the Thompsons' home.

Joanna and Mr Thompson were sitting side by side on an old lounge at one end of the verandah as Laura wheeled the motorbike up to the steps, Yogi panting at her heels.

'Hi, Mr Thompson. Hi, Joanna,' Laura said, knocking out the kickstand on the bike with her foot and placing her helmet on the seat.

'Joanna said you wanted to speak with me.' Arthur Thompson's voice was deep and sombre.

Laura nodded. 'I want to understand what happened at the gorge all those years ago.'

'Why?' he asked. 'Why's it so important to you?'

Laura drew the strap of a backpack over her head. 'I searched for records of an incident at the gorge. I have some documents. They show there was trouble between the Thompsons and an early settler named Jeremiah Pyke, but I haven't found any official account of the death of a man or baby at the gorge.' She had slipped the photocopied pages from her bag. Now she held them, gripped in trembling hands.

'I want to help you, Mr Thompson,' she went on. 'Show the town your family is good. That the old stories are true, but it was your ancestor who tried to stop the deaths of the convict and baby. I thought it might help if we get recognition for what George Thompson did, all those years ago.'

'Recognition? What do you mean?'

'Well, you know, get it on the official record. Published,' Laura muttered. 'It would mean more people would know the truth. And I … I want to know if you think the gorge is, well, haunted.'

Arthur Thompson surveyed two lorikeets cuddling in the tea tree for so long Laura was sure he was not interested and was going to tell her to leave. When he rose and headed inside the house, Laura cursed under her breath. Gran always said she tackled things like a bull at a gate. She was about to call out 'Thanks anyway' when the man turned and gestured for her to follow him.

Laura took the cue and hoisted her bag over her shoulder. Pausing at the door, she turned to Yogi. 'I'll be back soon. Stay,' she said as the dog lay down to wait.

While Joanna made a pot of tea, Laura handed over the photocopies: Anne Kelly's diary entry, the letter from Jeremiah Pyke to the governor, and the account from John Oxley. As Arthur read the documents, Laura placed her mobile phone on the table.

'Is it okay if I record you?'

After getting a nod of agreement, Laura checked that the voice recorder was working. Clearing her throat, she began: 'Thank you for your time, Mr Thompson. You're a descendant of George Thompson, an early settler who moved to Wallaby Rock around 1820. Is that right?'

'I am,' he replied.

'There's been stories circulating for years about a horrific death at a large cliff overlooking the gorge during those times. Could you please tell me what you know of this?'

'First, I can say that what my daughter Joanna told you is true. You need to understand that the relationship between the Thompsons and Pykes …' Arthur Thompson hesitated; he seemed to be searching for the right word. '… It was toxic. They were two families at war. Jeremiah Pyke, who owned land next to my ancestor – George Thompson – was allegedly a hothead. He had a terrible temper, and there were stories that he beat his convicts and even his wife. I have some copies of old letters that George wrote to family back in Ireland. My relatives living there kept them and sent them to my wife, Kathleen, when she contacted them seeking information about our family history. Kathleen was into that stuff. She wanted something for our kids to keep, to show where we came from.'

Arthur paused, and Laura figured he was struggling to talk about his wife.

'Would you be able to share those letters with me?' Laura prompted.

He nodded, getting up and disappearing into a bedroom at the end of the hall. Laura paused the recording, and the two girls chatted about school while they waited.

'Here you go,' Mr Thompson said, placing a shoebox on the table and handing over a few pieces of paper to Laura. 'These are a good place to start.'

Laura took the papers from him, her fingers tracing over words written so long ago.

12 August 1822

My dearest sister,

I trust all is well at home. Life in the colonies goes on. It is not easy, but Caroline and I work hard to succeed. This harsh land is like another world, as different from home as you could imagine.

The soil is hard and the sun is so hot it could melt the skin from your face. Working the farm has been difficult, but thankfully we have the river. I take what I can to keep my cattle and crops alive, but water is life and a point of contention with my neighbour, Jeremiah Pyke.

Mr Pyke is a cantankerous man, prone to fits of anger; I have never come across a more disagreeable person in my life.

Several times we've come close to blows. I'd hoped the friendship blossoming between our good wives, who are both expecting, might mend our relationship, but alas, nothing seems to temper his foul moods.

The rest of the letter talked about the pending birth of their child and hopes for the future. Laura resumed the voice recording.

'So, Mr Thompson,' Laura spoke to the phone, 'this letter from your ancestor, George Thompson, confirms that he and Mr Pyke fought with each other. Correct?'

'That's right. But things got worse. I think you'll find this more interesting,' Arthur replied, handing another wad of papers to Laura.

Laura skimmed the text and gasped as she got to the bottom of the first page. She looked up at Arthur. 'Would you mind if I read this out, for the recording?'

Arthur nodded.

10 December 1822

My dear sister,

I beg forgiveness. There is nothing to excuse my failure to correspond with those I love, but I hope when you read this you will understand why. I don't know how to put into words what has transpired these last months, but I will try to make sense of all that has occurred.

I told you of my neighbour, Jeremiah Pyke. Our troubles worsened when he accused Michael, a young convict in my employ, of having an affair with his wife, Maggie. Maggie was a regular visitor to our home, often taking refuge from her husband. She and Michael, being of similar age, struck up a friendship, but I swear on our mother's grave, I never knew of any dalliances.

Pyke stopped his wife from visiting us, and Caroline was wearing out her rosary beads, praying for the safety of the lass and the babe she carried.

Pyke ordered me to flog young Michael for daring to consort with his wife. I refused, and the next morning, I found several of my cattle dead, their throats slit. I confronted Pyke, and he refused to speak, instead aiming his musket at my head.

That night, there was a commotion in the worker's hut. Pyke, carrying his newborn child, dragged Michael out of bed and herded him through the bush.

Caroline begged me to take the musket, but I feared this would only enrage Pyke further. I ordered her to stay inside and left my men to protect her.

What I saw next will lie heavy on my heart forever.

Pyke had Michael and the baby at the edge of a cliff, telling the young man to jump or be shot. Pyke believed the child was Michael's. We fought and, in the struggle, I was knocked out. I was later told, to my own great despair, that Pyke pushed Michael and the babe over the edge to their deaths.

I was saved only by the arrival of Caroline and my men.

You may be wondering what happened to Jeremiah. I believe he perished in the scrub. No one has seen him since that fateful night at the cliff. Poor Maggie had died in childbirth, and Caroline and I buried her, the child, and young Michael.

I am recovering from my physical injuries, but a heavy weight lies on my heart and soul. I should have done more to help, should have disciplined Michael, and maybe this awful series of events would never have happened.

I have no more to share with you, my dearest. Please pray for me and our family.

George

Laura took a sip of tea before continuing. Gran always said a good cup of tea was the best tonic to calm the nerves.

'So, Mr Thompson, is this the reason you believe the gorge is haunted, that it may be cursed? Do you believe the stories are true? That it's the ghost of Michael and the baby that people sometimes hear and see?'

Arthur glanced at his daughter before responding. 'I do. I believe the gorge is a bad place, where awful things have happened … and keep happening. From his letter, it appears poor George blamed himself for what occurred. The Thompsons have had a lot of bad luck over the years, and there's been several incidents involving our family at that place. Just look at what happened to my wife, Kathleen, and to my sons.' Arthur's voice shook.

'It's okay, Dad. You don't have to say any more,' Joanna said, moving closer to her father.

Arthur pulled his daughter to his side and turned to Laura, nodding at her phone. Laura pushed the stop button on the recording and waited.

'Can I trust you, Laura? What I'm about to tell you must remain between us. It's not for any public story or newspaper article. Do you give me your word?'

Laura returned the man's steady gaze and nodded.

'My wife was troubled, at the end. She became obsessed with the story of Jeremiah Pyke, Michael, and the baby. She believed Jeremiah was talking to her, telling her to do things … to hurt herself. When Benny and Jordy were born, it got worse.

I tried to get her help, but she refused and got angry because she thought I didn't believe her. Then one night, she left the house and went to the cliff over the gorge. She left me a note, telling me she had to leave us or Jeremiah would hurt our children. She said it was an eye for an eye. A wife … for a wife.' Arthur's hands shook as he drank his tea.

His voice was barely more than a whisper as he continued, 'I burned the note before the police could find it. I didn't want the gossipers in this town to know how unwell Kathleen was. To judge her when she couldn't help what she was going through. I wanted to protect my wife and my family from that.'

Laura nodded once more. She'd been called crazy all her life; she could understand what Arthur had done.

There was so much to digest, and she didn't know how to approach the next bit of her questioning. She had no way of knowing if Joanna had shared the story of her dream with her father, and she didn't know how to bring it up after Mr Thompson had shared something so personal.

She looked up to see Arthur, his brown eyes so like Joanna's, staring hard at her, his hands wrapped around his cup of tea.

'I wondered … You know a woman was found murdered recently, in the gorge?' Laura looked from Joanna to her father.

'Yes, and the police are still investigating. How nice of them to keep on the job!'

Sucking in a deep breath, Laura dived in. 'Do you … do you think the gorge is haunted or cursed? All the deaths and disappearances over the last 200 years, do you think these are connected in some way to what happened to Michael and the baby? Do you think this is the reason bad things keep happening?'

Twisting his cup in his hands, Arthur examined the remains of his tea before responding. 'There's something wrong with that place. I do believe that the murder of Michael and the newborn triggered something, that this one event infected the land and set off a chain reaction.' Arthur's voice trembled as he continued. 'I should have left, after Kathleen, I should have known it wouldn't end but I couldn't leave. This property, what's left of it anyway, has been in our family for generations. I couldn't walk away and now it's too late. Too late to save Kathleen, and my boys.'

Laura's voice was soft and sincere. 'I can't understand what it's been like for you and Joanna – what you have gone through as a family. But that's why I think it's important your story, George's story, is heard. It might help others realise what good people the Thompsons are.'

'You won't change everyone's views, Laura, but you can try if you want to.' Arthur stood. 'I've said enough. Good luck with your research.'

Laura thanked Arthur and packed away her phone and documents.

'I don't know if it'll make any difference,' Joanna said as she walked Laura out to the verandah, 'but I'm glad Dad talked to you.'

Laura stood by the motorbike and kicked the stand up, preparing to leave. She was eager to be at home before her family returned, but she couldn't leave Joanna this way.

'You knew all this time, didn't you? About your mum. What she was struggling with. Why didn't you tell me?'

Joanna looked back at the house and then turned to Laura, her face wet with tears. 'I hate this place. Dad always told me Mum loved us. He said she was sick and couldn't help what happened. I knew she took her own life, but Dad never told me why. Not until Benny and Jordy died. I hate this place,' Joanna repeated.

Laura broke all the rules and hugged the one person who'd stood by her when everyone else had turned away. 'I'm sorry I've been a crap friend. I'm here for you, always.' The two pulled apart, and Laura shoved her helmet on her head and mounted the motorbike, the old engine spluttering to life.

'C'mon, Yogi. Let's go.'

'Wait!' Joanna cried, grabbing Laura in another hug, her embrace tight. 'Remember what I said, Laura. Stay away from that awful place. It's not safe.'

Chapter 14 – Laura

Laura followed the coverage of Yvette Berger's murder investigation with keen interest, but it was difficult as her mum kept turning off the TV and radio whenever the case was mentioned. Laura overheard her telling Gran that she kept picturing Sarah, who had worked at the orchard, as the victim. Laura resorted to following the story online.

Bit by bit, the police released more details surrounding Yvette's death. The young woman had been bashed in the head, stripped of her clothes, and hidden in a shallow grave about five kilometres downriver from where Benny and Jordy were discovered. To date, there were no concrete leads, and no one had been arrested for her murder.

The police questioned the orchard owner but made it clear he was not a suspect. The police also questioned Yvette's backpacker friends, but this had also turned up nothing. The last time anyone had seen Yvette was when she finished work for the day and headed into Wallaby Rock to do her shopping. It was Mr Sias who found Yvette's burnt-out old Kombi van on a secluded back road.

Contrary to what had been reported on the news, Yvette's family were waiting for approval to come to Australia and bring their daughter home. In the meantime, locals laid flowers and cards at the site of her bush grave. The media were in a frenzy, dubbing the murderer the 'Bush Basher'. The sensationalist moniker renewed interest in the Thompson case, but the police were under intense pressure to rule out any connection between the deaths. Senator Thompson was leading the call for the police to put more resources into the boys' case.

It became almost impossible to sneak away for bushwalks and to visit Joanna. Jeannie had decided, even with Yogi's protection, it wasn't safe for Laura to wander the bush on her own and wanted to know where she was every minute of the day.

The time had come to talk to her parents about her ongoing friendship with Joanna and her discussion with Mr Thompson. Her parents knew Laura had been friends with the Thompson children growing up but were not aware she had maintained a close bond with Joanna and trained with the family. Growing up, Laura had relished the freedom of visiting and training with the Thompsons whenever she wanted to. While she was now legally an adult, she hoped her past actions wouldn't fracture her relationship with her parents in any way, having hidden things from them for so long.

Deciding to talk first to Gran, Laura waited until she was in the garden weeding and pruning her beloved roses.

Pulling on a pair of gardening gloves, Laura knelt beside Grace, grasped a bunch of prickly weeds, and yanked them out of the flowerbed.

'You know it's amazing I have any roses left. Your grandfather thinks it's funny when the wombats eat them – I've tried fencing my roses off and covering them, but the wombats keep coming back.'

'Gran, you know the information we found at the State Library?' Laura began.

Grace hummed a reply as she clipped six crimson roses from the garden.

'I know more about it.'

'Do you?' Grace kept up the war on weeds.

'Do you know Arthur Thompson?' Laura asked.

'Yes, of course.' Grace stopped gardening and turned to face her granddaughter.

'Umm … I know his daughter. We were friends in primary school, and Joanna sprints too. I asked Joanna if I could talk to her father about the information we uncovered, and he agreed to speak to me.'

'And …?' Grace asked over Laura's grunts as she wrestled the stubborn weeds from the rock-hard ground.

'I spoke to him,' Laura huffed. 'Her dad said there was a feud between the Thompsons and Pykes. He told me Jeremiah Pyke murdered a young convict who was working for the Thompsons. Jeremiah believed the man had an affair with his wife. He pushed him, with Jeremiah's newborn child, over the big cliff and into the gorge. Mr Thompson thinks the gorge is haunted and cursed.'

Laura tossed weeds to one side as she continued. 'I spoke to my history teacher, Mr Herbert, and he said it would be a good research piece for my final assignment and that he may know someone from Sydney University who would be interested in the information.'

Grace trimmed leaves from the cut roses. 'If you're close to Joanna, were you close to her brothers too?'

Laura threw another weed onto her growing pile. 'I've been friends with Joanna and her brothers since primary school, and we stayed friends. We trained together – you know, sprint training – before the boys died.'

Grace removed her gardening gloves. 'Why didn't you tell us this before, Laura? I take it your mum and dad don't know?'

'No, they don't. Joanna is a good friend, and I *liked* Benny and Jordy.' Laura's voice caught in her throat.

Grace patted her granddaughter's arm. 'They'll understand, Laura. Just talk to them.' The pair stood and carried the roses inside. Grace arranged them in a vase on top of the piano in the sitting room.

***

Laura waited until after dinner to talk to her parents. They were stretched out on the lounge waiting for *Home and Away* to come on. It was her mum's favourite show.

Grace sat in the corner knitting; her eyes fixed on the screen. Jack was in the kitchen doling out ice cream and chocolate topping into bowls.

'Mum and Dad, you know Mr Thompson?' Laura began.

Henry and Jeannie nodded.

'I visited him the other day for my major history assignment. I asked him about early settlement and what life was like for his ancestors. Mr Thompson shared a story about the killing of one of his convicts and a baby, at the gorge. He showed me old family letters that tie the murders to another early settler, Jeremiah Pyke. What he told me lines up with the information Gran and I turned up at the State Library.'

Henry and Jeannie turned to each other. Her father spoke first. 'When did you speak to Mr Thompson?'

'Last weekend. I know him through his daughter, Joanna. Do you remember Joanna? She was my friend in primary school, along with his sons, Benny and Jordy. We all trained together. Sprint training at their place. Joanna and I used to train at lunchtime at school, and after she moved to Wallaby Rock High, we kept training, but at her place. That's how I know Mr Thompson. He hasn't been feeling too good lately. I hoped talking about what happened might help.'

Laura saw the hurt on her father's face. 'I'm sorry, Dad. I know you wanted to help me train, but you never had enough time. I didn't want to keep hassling you about it. You and Grandad are always so busy with the farm, and I understand. It's okay. I get it. The farm comes first. Besides, Mr Thompson set up racing lanes out the back, so, you know, it was just easy to train with them.'

'First, you sneak out and break COVID rules. Second, you keep your friendship with the Thompsons a secret for years. Why? Did you think we wouldn't let you be friends or train with them? Contrary to what some people say, Mr Thompson is a decent man. Then Benny and Jordy died, and still, you didn't tell us?' Jack stopped in the doorway carrying two bowls overloaded with ice cream as Henry's voice grew louder. 'Do you think we listen to idle gossip? Do you think so little of us?'

'No. No,' Laura said, her voice wavering. 'I just … I don't know. I wanted to do my own thing. Being confined to the farm has been driving me nuts. I miss Joanna. She is one of my only friends, and the training was important to me. I'm sorry.'

'We know you're an adult, Laura, and can make your own decisions, but no matter how old you are, we want you to feel like you can talk to us – not hide things from your family. Do you understand?' Henry asked, his blue eyes locked on Laura's.

Laura nodded; she sucked in a deep breath, then exhaled. 'There's more.'

'Go on,' Henry said, cutting off Jeannie, who'd opened her mouth to interject.

'The night before Benny and Jordy were discovered, I dreamt of them. They were in the gorge and were being followed by someone. To the bridge. The next morning, I went to the waterhole and saw the images from my dream again. I went to the bridge and saw blood on the rocks. The police were there, and I hid – I didn't want to explain what I'd dreamt to anyone. I didn't think anyone would believe me, or they'd think I was … you know … disturbed or something, so I kept it to myself. And the story about Joanna's ancestor and the killing at the gorge? I dreamt of that too. I was there and saw it happening. Mr Thompson thinks the gorge is tainted, that the country has been infected because of that terrible event. I think he believes his family is cursed because his ancestor failed to stop the murders.' Laura hestitated. She'd given her word to Arthur and wouldn't betray his confidence about his wife. 'But I've been thinking. Maybe I'm cursed or a bad person. I mean, how can I love going to the gorge so much when it's such a bad place? A place where such terrible things have happened. I've even wondered if, perhaps, our ancestors, the Murrays, could've stepped in and helped end the fighting between the families but didn't, and that's why I see these things. Perhaps these dreams are a punishment for our family not taking action.'

It was Jack, not Henry, who responded. 'You're not defective or cursed or being punished. You're *special*, Laura.' Jack placed the bowls on the side table and motioned to Grace. 'Like your grandmother and great-grandmother. Isn't that right, Grace?'

Grace rose from her armchair and took Jack's hand. 'That's right, Laura. The gift of sight runs in *my* family, not your grandfather's. So, it can't be a punishment or curse for anything the Murrays did or didn't do in the past.'

'The Murrays were one of the few families here at that time. Surely Frederick Murray would have known and could have done something?' Laura turned to Jack and Henry. 'I need to know.'

Jack let go of Grace's hand and balanced himself on the arm of the lounge next to Laura, rubbing her back to calm her down like when she was little. 'There's no mention of it, love, not in any of our family journals or letters. Your grandmother's been through all of them over the years. I'm not saying Frederick wouldn't have known about the feud – he probably did – but whether he could have helped or not? We'll never know.'

Laura chewed at her bottom lip, and Jack continued. 'We can't change the past, but we can shape the future. What you're doing for Joanna and Arthur Thompson, that's a good thing, Laura.'

***

The following day, Mr Herbert asked Laura to stay online after class.

'Exciting news, Laura. My friend, Professor Smith, at Sydney University would like to talk to your friend's father, Mr Thompson,' Mr Herbert stuttered, eager to share the news with her.

Laura thought about Mr Thompson and his reluctance to meet with or share his story with outsiders. 'Does he have to talk to him? Can't he use what I already have?'

'He needs to interview Mr Thompson himself,' Mr Herbert explained. 'To verify your report. Joshua is a professor of Australian History, and he is working on a big paper. If it gets published, it will shed light on many untold stories from early settlement.'

'I think Mr Thompson only spoke to me as a favour to his daughter. He's a shy, reserved man. I'll need to check if he's happy to be interviewed,' Laura said.

'Good idea. Let me know what he says.' Mr Herbert's head was bouncing up and down as he smiled at her.

'I'd better go. I don't want to be late for my next class,' Laura said as she logged out of the virtual classroom.

Chapter 15 – Mick

Sergeant Mick Peters sat at his desk, flicking through the Yvette Berger file. It was getting late; he'd sent his offsider, Bob, home three hours ago.

A mug of coffee sat in front of him. It was stone cold. He contemplated making a fresh one but knew drinking caffeine late at night was a bad idea. His wife, Shirley, hated it when he didn't sleep, but this case was always on his mind. Mick felt he was missing something; the final clue was obscured and out of reach.

Scattered across his desk were photos of the burnt-out Kombi and Yvette's shallow grave. The images triggered unwelcome memories of the smell of burnt rubber, petrol, and damp earth.

They had no murder weapon, and Yvette's clothing and handbag were still missing. All their questioning had led to naught. Quite simply, they were no closer to chasing down the killer. The NSW Homicide Squad had taken over responsibility for the case. Detective Dave Graham was leading the investigation and working closely with Mick. Dave was one of the top homicide detectives in the force and had recently spent six months in an exchange with the FBI, in America, studying the latest criminal investigation techniques.

Mick examined the photos of Yvette's body for what felt like the hundredth time. As well as being bashed in the head,

Yvette had been sexually assaulted. They hadn't shared those details with the media. It was Dave's idea to withhold this vital piece of information to see how the killer would react – if it would make him angry, more reckless, or more careless. Maybe he'd trip up, make a mistake. Mick's daughter was seventeen, only a few years younger than Yvette, and whenever he stared at the photos of the victim, he saw his precious Claire.

Yvette's family in Germany constantly wanted updates on the case. The anger and frustration he felt for the Bergers, and his town, was palpable. He didn't want this on his watch. He couldn't have it. He opened a drawer and pulled out the file on the Thompson boys for the umpteenth time.

They had to be connected. There were too many similarities. The first was the severe trauma to the head. The forensics team had found multiple rock fragments around the head wounds in both cases. From the shape and angle of the trauma inflicted on the skulls of the three victims, forensics had determined a heavy, sharp, and uneven object, like a large rock, had been used with immense force on Yvette and the boys.

The location of the bodies was the other significant indicator that the same person may be responsible. The boys were discovered under the bridge at the bottom of the gorge. Yvette was in a shallow grave five kilometres away, close to the river that dissected the gorge.

There were, however, inconsistencies. Benny and Jordy had not been sexually assaulted and were still clothed when discovered. It appeared the killer preferred women – Mick remained convinced the same person was responsible for the deaths of Yvette and the Thompson boys.

Why Benny and Jordy? While the rest of the Thompson family was not well-regarded, the boys had no enemies. They were popular kids. Could they have disturbed the killer as he stalked or attacked someone else? If they had, could Mick expect to find more victims out there? The thought churned his stomach. There had been no missing person reports in the district. Could the killer be searching for victims outside the local area? People went missing all the time. Mick knew many people who went missing never wanted to be found, while others met with untimely and grisly ends.

He rubbed his hand across his forehead. He now had a splitting headache, and he didn't want coffee. All he wanted was to go home and hug his wife and daughter. He closed the files and locked them away, turned off the lights, and locked the office. As he climbed into the patrol car, he pulled the rear-view mirror down and stared hard at his reflection. He traced the lines around his eyes. Were there always so many? He touched the puffy bags that made him look like a fat toad. He'd aged. A lot. And he felt the way he looked – old and tired. This case was doing his head in.

***

The following morning, Mick called Dave.

'Hi, Dave. Any updates on the Berger case?' He hoped his colleague would claim to have had an amazing breakthrough overnight.

'Nothing new, Mick. Don't worry, mate. I'll let you know if we get any leads. You got anything for me?' he asked.

'I was thinking last night that there must be a connection between the Thompson and Berger cases. The head trauma, the close location of the victims – it fits.'

'Hang on, Mick. We've discussed this. I agree there are some similarities, but there are also inconsistencies in the two cases. You know there's no evidence of sexual assault in the Thompson case, and those boys were visible under the bridge. They weren't hidden or in a shallow grave like Berger.'

'But what if the two boys were victims of the same killer by mistake?' Mick dared. 'What if it was an opportunistic attack, or Benny and Jordy discovered something about the killer or even disturbed him stalking or attacking someone else? Perhaps the killer tried to pass their death off as an accident but failed. He could have staged it to put us off the scent. I mean, it's not impossible, is it?' Mick asked.

Dave paused before responding. 'Mick, we haven't got a strong lead for either case. It feels like we're chasing shadows.'

Mick pushed his point. 'But if it's true, there may be other bodies out there, or I potentially have a killer just waiting to take another victim – a murderer lurking in my backyard.'

'Okay, I get it,' Dave conceded. 'We'll review the evidence again in both cases and test your theories.'

'Appreciate it, Dave. Let me know how you go.'

Mick hung up, unlocked his drawer, and took out his files, placing the photos of the bodies of Benny, Jordy, and Yvette beside each other.

There had to be a clue. 'Who are you? Where are you?' he murmured to the photos.

Chapter 16 – Laura

Joanna and Laura met at the shops. Laura had come into town with Grace for groceries. While Gran chatted to her hairdresser outside Mrs Old Bags, Laura spied Joanna snatching something from the cantankerous shopkeeper and shoving it into the back pocket of her jeans.

'Hey, Joanna!' Laura said, eyeing Mrs Old Bags. 'Let's go outside.' The pair walked off, taking shelter in the shade of a large gum tree. 'I'm glad I saw you. I was hoping to speak to you and your dad.'

'What about this time?' Joanna looked past Laura to a spot in the distance.

'Remember me saying I wanted to help your dad get his story heard?'

'Yeah, why?'

'My history teacher, he knows a guy at Sydney University – a professor – who wants to document what happened. He talked about publishing your dad's story, but he needs to talk to him first,' Laura said, trying to gauge Joanna's reaction.

'About the story of the gorge?'

'Yeah. If it gets published, then everyone will know what your ancestor did. How he tried to help.'

'I've gotta go. Come over tomorrow afternoon? That will give me a chance to talk to him,' Joanna said.

'Thanks, Joanna. See ya,' Laura said.

'See ya.' Joanna strode away with a flick of her hair and a wave of one hand.

Not until Joanna left did Laura realise what had seemed different. Joanna Thompson … with her hair nice, and wearing make-up? The faint aroma of tobacco and alcohol lingered in the air. Laura assumed Joanna was meeting her boyfriend and the popular footy crew. Maybe they were even going to a party. Public gatherings and events were not allowed, but rules had never stopped Joanna Thompson from doing what she wanted.

Laura strolled back to the shop to wait for Gran, who was still in an animated conversation with her hairdresser. She overheard Shazza describing the police as incompetent bozos and heard Grace's diplomatic reply before wandering into the store and picking up a magazine. The pretty model on the cover had a pouty expression, flawless skin, big breasts, and immaculate make-up. Laura tossed it back on the stand with disgust.

***

Laura spent the next morning with Yogi. She hadn't taught him anything new in over a year and decided it was time to get back into his training. It was something that would keep them both occupied.

The idea for the trick came to her a few weeks ago after suffering through another no-meat-except-on-Fridays lent period, but she hadn't had time to put it into practice. In her head, she'd dubbed it the 'Catholic Dog Trick'.

Laura placed one piece of dry food in her hand and held it out for Yogi to take each time she called out the days of the week. When she got to Friday, she closed her hand and shook her head. She said the words, 'The Good Lord said you can eat meat,' and opened her hand for Yogi to take the kibble. It took most of the morning before she was able to keep her hand open and for Yogi to wait for the magic words before taking the food. Laura was excited to show her family what Yogi had learned. She'd forgotten how much she loved working with her pet. As she got older, she'd stopped teaching him new tricks, and now she remembered how much they both enjoyed it. He always wanted to please her, and his strong food drive made rewards the perfect motivation to learn new tricks. She also took great pride in how smart he was. Cuddling her dog, she told him how clever he was before going inside to tell her mother she was expected at Joanna's.

She told Jeannie she needed to speak with the Thompsons about the interest from Sydney University in their story. Her mother wanted her to call them, reminding her daughter that she should avoid visiting other people, but Laura insisted that she needed to talk to Mr Thompson face-to-face and promised to wear a mask and keep her distance. Then Jeannie wanted to drive her, but Laura said she'd take the car with Yogi and wouldn't be long, her primary reason being that too many people might unsettle Mr Thompson, who was a very private person. Finally, Jeannie agreed.

After Laura had confessed to her friendship and training with the Thompsons, her parents had agreed to treat her as a grown-up, but with that, they expected her to be open and honest with them. Laura knew it was hard for her mother, who couldn't bear to think of her baby as a young woman and was having trouble letting go. And she knew Jeannie was worried about her hanging out with Joanna. She heard her parents discussing it late one night as she crept to the kitchen for a glass of water. Laura heard her father reassuring her mother that she was sensible and could be a good influence on Joanna. Henry finished by reinforcing that the Thompsons needed a friend.

As Laura stepped out of the car to open the gate, she noticed the garden was tidier, and someone had cut the grass. Laura took this as a good sign. While she didn't fully comprehend the distinct phases of grief or the deep impact the loss of a parent, child, brother, or sister could have, Laura was wise enough to know the sudden death of Benny and Jordy had changed both Mr Thompson's and Joanna's lives forever.

She parked the car under the tea tree and walked up the steps to the front door, Yogi by her side. The main door was open and the screen door appeared unlocked. She knocked and called out to let them know she was there, and Joanna poked her head around the side of the house.

'Hi, Laura. We're out the back,' Joanna said, waving her over.

As Laura and Yogi turned the corner, Arthur was sitting on a chair on the rear verandah, a beer in his hand, gazing at the paddocks. Was he looking at the racing lanes? Remembering happier times? The lanes were there, somewhere under the long grass. It was clear Joanna wasn't training.

'Hello, Laura,' Arthur said in his deep voice. 'Joanna said you wanted to talk to me again?'

Laura sat on the edge of the verandah, and Yogi waited for her to tell him to sit before he settled at her feet.

'That's a good dog you have there,' Arthur said.

'He's clever. He does tricks, you know. I taught him a new one. Do you want to see it? I'll need a bit of meat.'

Joanna responded to her dad's nod and walked into the house, returning with a chunk of mince, which she handed to Laura. Yogi sat to attention, his eyes never leaving Laura.

'We only worked on this one today, so he may not get it right the first time,' she said.

Breaking the mince into small pieces, Laura placed a portion in her right hand and led Yogi through each day of the week, just like they'd practised. Yogi executed the trick to perfection.

'Good boy,' she exclaimed while Arthur laughed and cheered, calling Yogi to his side for a pat.

'Isn't he a clever boy, Joanna?' Arthur said, unaware the daughter standing behind him was smiling.

Guessing there hadn't been much laughter in their home, Laura grinned back, glad she and Yogi had brightened their day a little.

Arthur settled back in his chair. 'Now, what did you want to talk to me about, Laura? Is it about George and the story of the gorge?'

Laura nodded as she leaned back against the railing. 'Do you remember when I said I wanted to document what happened there? Well, there's this history professor, from Sydney University, who needs to speak to you before he can use your story. I said I needed to check with you first as you may not be comfortable talking to him,' Laura explained.

Mr Thompson was still and silent, staring again at the paddocks overgrown with weeds.

Laura looked sideways at Joanna, seeking her support and approval to continue. Turning back to face Arthur, she found him looking right at her.

'You're Henry Murray's daughter,' he stated. Laura nodded, swallowing hard. 'Your family has been on that farm for a long time.'

'Yes, they have. And to be honest, one reason I want to help is I don't know if the Murrays could have helped to end the feud between the Thompsons and Pykes. Maybe they couldn't have done anything anyway, but knowing they were living here at the same time … Well, maybe they could've helped but chose not to. That makes me sad. I can't change the past, but I can help shine a light on what took place all those years ago.'

Arthur finished the rest of his beer and tossed it in the bin, the sound of glass clinking hinted at a full container of empty stubbies. He turned to his daughter. 'You have a good friend, Joanna.' He gave Yogi a rub around the ears as he spoke to Laura. 'I'll talk to this Professor Smith. You can give him our phone number.'

With that, Mr Thompson grabbed what was left of his six-pack and went inside, leaving Joanna, Laura, and Yogi on the back porch.

'Hey, Joanna,' Laura said, her gaze fixed on the overgrown racing lanes. 'The state championships aren't far away. I have a set of starting blocks at home, and Dad's been helping me train on weekends. You're welcome to join us.'

Joanna shrugged. 'Thanks, but I'm busy with other stuff. I've gotta go.' Joanna gave Yogi a final pat before she headed inside.

As she drove home with the windows down to let in fresh air for Yogi, Laura was so deep in thought she didn't pay any attention to the white ute that slowed after she passed it.

Laura stopped at the entrance to the Murray farm, getting out to unlock the gate. Yogi jumped out to run the rest of the way to the house, like he always did. But as she pulled up next to the garage, she realised Yogi was still sitting at the entrance, watching the road. She whistled, and her beloved pooch came running to her side.

Chapter 17 – Laura

September 2020

Laura's final assignments, prepping for exams, and her training sucked up all her spare time. It was September. The state championships were just a week away and there was only a month left before the start of the Higher School Certificate exams and the end of her school life. Laura and her classmates had started attending classes at the school again now that COVID restrictions had lightened a bit. Considering the year she'd had, Laura reckoned she deserved an award for simply getting through high school.

While considered by teachers as bright and curious, Laura would never be top of the class. She struggled to put in the effort she needed with subjects she didn't like, and the events over the last year had been a serious distraction. Right now, she was busy studying biology, getting her mother to quiz her in the sitting room.

'How'd I go this time, Mum?' Laura asked.

'Not too bad,' Jeannie said. 'I marked the things you got wrong so you can go over them.'

Laura silently thanked God that she hadn't stuffed up her revision – she'd never hear the end of it, otherwise.

Handing over her notes, Jeannie asked, 'Are you still trying to get into veterinary science? Do you think you need a backup plan, just in case?'

Laura looked down. There were more red crosses than ticks on the pages, and her heart sank. Her mother was trying to keep her spirits up. 'I want to try. I know the marks I need are high, but it's what I want to do. If I don't get into that, I'll think about what I do next.' Laura tried not to let Jeannie see how much it meant to her to become a vet.

'Well, keep studying, and you'll get there,' her mother said, handing over the revision sheet with an encouraging smile.

***

The next day, Laura received a B+ for her essay on Miles Franklin's *My Brilliant Career*. It was the best mark she'd received in English all year. Laura had enjoyed the book, finding it easy to relate to Sybylla's independent and headstrong ways and her desire to pursue her path and purpose in life. What was even better was overhearing her teacher berating Liv Hansen for her lack of effort and poor-quality work.

Laura was in a good mood and chatted with the driver, George, on the bus trip home. Jeannie was waiting for her at the bus stop as usual.

As she clambered into the car, Laura noticed the radio was off, and Jeannie was clutching at the steering wheel like it was a lifeline. Something was up. Her mother always listened to the *ABC News* and talkback and would often shush Laura on the drive home.

'Hi, Mum,' Laura said, settling in the front passenger seat and buckling her seat belt.

'Hello, Laura,' Jeannie said.

Laura couldn't wait to share her good news. 'Hey, I got a B+ for my English essay,' she said and waited for her mother's reaction.

'That's nice,' said Jeannie as she waited for the bus to leave.

She'd gotten a B+ and all her mother had to say was 'That's nice'? A high mark would normally elicit a much better response.

'Mum, is everything okay?' Laura asked as Jeannie hit the car's blinker with excessive force.

'There's been another disappearance,' Jeannie admitted. 'A seventeen-year-old girl from the high school is missing. Your father and grandfather are helping the police with the search this evening. We'll all have to help with the milking so they can get away early.'

Laura chewed at her bottom lip. 'Who is it?'

'Mia Stevens.'

Laura gasped. It felt like a vice tightening across her heart. She knew Mia. She was pretty and popular and had been a year below her in primary school. Her father worked for the Department of Main Roads, and her mother volunteered at the primary school.

Jeannie turned to her daughter, holding her gaze. 'Laura, I'm worried; so is your father. No more wandering off alone. It's not safe.'

Chapter 18 – Henry

Henry parked the farm ute along the road near the town hall a few minutes after five. A line of cars, utes, and four-wheel drives were parked down the street as locals gathered for the search party briefing. Among the vehicles was a van with '*National Nightly News*' plastered on the side, and Henry recognised the reporter, John Gordon, who was directing his cameraman to film locals as they entered the hall for the briefing. Gordon was holding a microphone, notepad, and mobile phone, and a pen poked out from behind his left ear. As Sergeant Peters pulled up, the journalist hurried over, and Henry watched as the senior policeman pulled the reporter aside. After several minutes of animated conversation, the pair shook hands, and the crew moved to the back of the hall to film proceedings.

Henry hadn't spoken a word to Jack as they drove to the briefing. He was too angry. Before he left, he and Laura had a furious argument, ending in Laura storming to her room in tears. She'd wanted to come with them, to help in the search for Mia, but Henry had forbidden it. She couldn't afford time out from studying for her final exams. And what if she found Mia or discovered some trace of her? He didn't know if Laura was ready for that. He didn't know if *he* was ready for that.

'Hey, mate,' Henry said to Jim, who ran the pub, as they entered the hall. Henry nodded to friends and neighbours as he grabbed two fold-up chairs, and he and Jack took their seats. Stowing a torch under his chair, he did a quick head count. 'Good turnout,' he whispered to Jack.

He estimated there were more than forty men and women gathered, waiting to hear from Sergeant Peters and the head of the Wallaby Rock State Emergency Service (SES), Jeremy Simpson.

The low murmur of quiet conversation petered out as Mick and Jeremy stepped onto the stage at the front of the hall. Beside them was a female mannequin wearing a blonde wig and dressed in the Wallaby Rock High School uniform, with a bag sitting next to the figure. Henry felt himself tearing up as he imagined the pain Mia's family must be going through.

Mick cleared his throat, and Henry leaned forward in his chair.

'Good evening and thank you for coming,' Mick began in a loud voice. 'As you have heard, seventeen-year-old Mia Stevens has been reported missing by her family. Mia visited her friend's house, the Jenkins residence on Oak Street, after school yesterday and left shortly before five o'clock to walk home. It's around two kilometres from the Jenkins residence to Mia's home on Gumtree Road, near the northern end of town. Mia has shoulder-length blonde hair and blue eyes and is around 170 centimetres, or five foot seven. She was last seen wearing her uniform and carrying a bag like this one.' Mick held up the black Billabong backpack that had been sitting beside the mannequin.

'We have copies of a recent photo of Mia, enough for each of you; Bob will hand these out before you head off tonight,' Mick said, pointing to Senior Constable Bob Fowler, who was standing at the back of the hall. 'I will now hand over to Jeremy, who will talk you through the search procedure for this evening.' Mick stepped back, and SES Chief, Jeremy Simpson, paused, taking in the locals who had gathered to help with the search.

Henry and Jack often helped with SES operations and shared a beer or two with Jeremy and his crew. Henry noticed Jeremy pulling at the edge of his sleeve. He knew Jeremy well enough to recognise this was a sign his friend was nervous or stressed.

Clearing his throat, Jeremy addressed the volunteers. 'Mia is one of our kids. We all know her family, and we owe it to them to do a thorough job.' Henry nodded along with many others in the hall. 'There is a possibility Mia has been injured and has been unable to seek help, and we hold out hope we will find her safe. I cannot emphasise enough that time is critical in a search operation like this.'

Jeremy talked them through the procedures and protocols for the evening: some were tasked with door-knocking the area while others were assigned grid points to search in the surrounding bush.

The sound of chairs scraping and people shuffling filled the hall. Henry saw Sergeant Peters move to where John Gordon and other reporters were waiting to interview him.

Jack and Henry stood up, folded their chairs, and stacked them with the others in a pile at the back of the hall. They were assigned to one of the groups appointed to search the bushland near Gumtree Road. The leader of their group was a long-serving member of the SES. She took charge and briefed them on the area they would be searching and how the search would be conducted. The other members of their group were the publican, Jim; Arthur Thompson; local mechanic, Shane McLeod; two neighbours; and 'pub acquaintance' Gary Wilson, who worked at the nearby coal mine. Two of Gary's colleagues had also joined the team.

Henry noticed Arthur shuffling and staring at the ground as person after person approached him, shaking his hand and thanking him for taking part in the search. He overheard them saying how hard it must be for Arthur to help out after the loss of his sons. Arthur looked like a nervous horse ready to bolt at any moment, and Henry kept glancing at him as they methodically searched their section of the bush.

It was the first time Henry had spoken to Arthur since Benny and Jordy had died, and since Laura had confided in her ongoing friendship with the Thompsons. Henry knew the operation would be bringing back painful memories of Arthur's search for his sons, but there was no opportunity to catch up while they worked. They focused on the task at hand. As the sun set, they switched on their torches and the pace of search slowed as they tried to make sure nothing was missed.

At 9 pm, they took a short break. Their group had completed a full sweep of the bush next to Gumtree Road and was waiting for further directions.

Henry and Arthur sat on the edge of the road, enjoying a hot coffee and sandwiches supplied by the Country Women's Association as they took a breather. 'How're you going, Arthur? I haven't spoken to you since the boys passed away. I'm sorry for you and your daughter,' Henry said, engaging Arthur in their first real conversation of the evening.

Henry saw Arthur flinch when he mentioned the boys, but Henry pushed on. 'Laura told me she talked to you the other day.'

Arthur smiled as he turned to face Henry. 'She's a kind person. She cares about people. Not everyone does, you know.'

'She's a good kid,' Henry agreed, filled with pride. He leaned towards Arthur, lowering his voice. 'Laura told me about your ancestor and the gorge. She said some university bloke wants to talk to you. Have you spoken to him yet?'

'I was going to speak to him this weekend. Not sure if I can right now. Not with everything going on,' Arthur whispered.

'I understand, mate,' Henry said as they sat together watching the buzz of activity around them. 'Hopefully, he'll be able to get your story out there.'

Arthur shrugged, and they made their way to a table laden with hot urns and tins of instant coffee to top up their brews before their team leader waved them over for further instructions.

The search was called off around 11.30 pm, and Jack and Henry climbed, exhausted, into the old ute. The two men knew they'd only have a couple of hours of sleep before they had to get up again for the milking, but they'd still signed up to help with the search the following day.

Gary Wilson, who had been scouring the bushland alongside Jack, waved as he opened the door of his white Hilux parked nearby. 'See you tomorrow night, Jack,' Gary called.

'See ya tomorrow,' Jack replied.

Chapter 19 – Laura

Laura slammed the door to her room so hard that the windows shook. Heaving with anger, she threw herself on the bed, pummelling her fists into her pillow.

'I'm not a child,' she raged. She hadn't lost her temper like this since she was little. The realisation she was behaving like a three-year-old hit home, and she focused on slowing her breathing.

After calming down, she rose from the messy bed and pulled her study chair from the desk to the wardrobe. Balancing on the edge of the chair, she stretched out, her fingers reaching for a box perched on top of the cupboard. Standing on her toes, her fingers grasped cardboard, dragging the box down. Books, trophies and cards fell to the floor as she stumbled off the chair holding the box to her chest. Amongst the mess, Laura spied the footy card she found at the waterhole, the one that had belonged to Benny and Jordy. Picking it up, she placed it next to the box on the bed.

After blowing dust off a collection of old toys, books, and comics, she found it. Lowering herself to the floor, Laura leaned against the edge of the bed as she opened the album.

Her face grinned at her, the colour fading from candid snapshots of birthdays and Christmases when she and Sarah were babies and small children. Flicking the pages, she found what she was looking for – a photo from the sports carnival in her final year of primary school. Chest out, she proudly displayed the ribbons she'd won. Next to her, Joanna held aloft a trophy; she'd been crowned school champion. To one side, Benny and Jordy wrestled on the ground, and a smaller girl with blonde plaits and a pretty face laughed at their antics. Mia.

Mia had been in her home group, the same athletics and swimming team as Laura. While popular, she hadn't teased or picked on Laura, but she hadn't stopped others from doing it either.

Laura pulled the photo out and stared at the face of the girl who was now missing. She remembered her mother taking the photo. Could remember it like it was yesterday.

It was September, early spring, and it had been warmer than usual. They'd been blessed with a bright, sunny day for the carnival, but staring closer at the photo, Laura noticed long, thin, dark shadows stretching from the corner of the picture and touching Benny, Jordy, and Mia. No big deal, except they were in the middle of the oval. There were no trees or buildings to cast any shadow.

She dropped the photo as if it had burned her. Why hadn't she noticed it before? Gran could see messages in the tea leaves. Was this a warning she should have heeded?

***

That evening, Laura, Grace, and Jeannie tuned into the news. They listened to Sergeant Peters describe Mia's appearance and recount her last known whereabouts before the policeman called on the public to come forward with any information that could help with the search and investigation. In the news report, John Gordon wrapped up by highlighting the recent deaths in Wallaby Rock before speculating the same person may be connected to all three cases.

Laura read every online news report she could and watched a string of Mia's friends on Snapchat and TikTok sobbing and pleading with anyone who knew anything to help the police with their search. Every call for help was tagged with #BringMiaHome. She waited until she heard the ute lumbering up the drive, then clambered out of bed. She waited in her doorway for her father.

'Laura, what're you still doing up?' Henry asked, rubbing dirt from his face as he made his way to the bathroom.

'I wanted to apologise. I'm sorry, Dad. I shouldn't have lost my temper today,' Laura said, stepping forward to embrace her father.

Lifting Laura's head from his chest, Henry looked into her eyes. 'It's okay, darl. I'm sorry I raised my voice. It's not something I want you to deal with. You're still my little girl, you know.'

'I know, Dad. Did you find Mia? Any sign of her?'

Henry shook his head. 'No, love. Nothing. But we'll keep going. I'm sure we'll find her soon.'

Laura nodded and hugged her father again before returning to her room.

Reaching under her pillow, she pulled out the photo of Mia and the West Tigers footy card. Sitting up, she prayed as she used to when she was little, like Gran had taught her. She asked Saint Patrick to return Mia to them, alive and well. Her fingers ran over the image of her friends, Benny and Jordy, and she asked the Irish saint to make sure the boys found their way to him, in heaven.

That night, she dreamed she was sprinting, dodging shadows that shot from the sky like lightning strikes. Legs pumping, she raced across the paddocks of the farm, Yogi panting beside her. She ran to the cliff, her feet skidding to a stop just centimetres from the edge before she lost her balance, toppling over the cliff face as screams filled the air.

Chapter 20 – Laura

Wallaby Rock, a quiet town few people had ever heard of, was now on the front pages of every major newspaper and a hot story on social media. But it wasn't the type of fame anyone in the district had ever wanted.

The *National Nightly News* ran a special television feature called *The Little Town with a Dark History*. The show was so popular it was recut and replayed on a national true crime podcast. Hosted by John Gordon, the program highlighted the high number of deaths and odd occurrences in Wallaby Rock since white settlement. The story included images and old newspaper reports of Captain Jack – a notorious bushranger who raided the stagecoaches and harassed property owners.

Standing at Captain Jack's grave in the old Wallaby Rock cemetery, John Gordon reflected on the outlaw's exploits being romanticised over time, yet his kill list was long and his deeds included the brutal murders of women and children. Reading from records unearthed from the State Library in Sydney, Gordon described, in detail, Captain Jack's gruesome method of tying mortally wounded and naked men to fallen trees full of bull ants, where they slowly died from their wounds while being stung multiple times by the colony defending its nest.

Gordon also reported on the high number of other disappearances in the area. One of the most perplexing and well-known was that of eight-year-old Joey Evans.

In 1951, Joey disappeared without a trace from his family's Wallaby Rock property after telling his mother he was going out to play. The search for Joey dragged on for months. Suspects at the time included Joey's father and a hitchhiker who had been passing through on his way to Melbourne. Both were later cleared. Joey's body was never found, and no murder charges were ever laid. The case remained unsolved.

John Gordon's report moved to more recent events: the suspected murder of rising football stars Benny and Jordy Thompson; the murder of Yvette Berger; and the search for local teenager, Mia Stevens. Gordon hypothesised about links between all three cases and ran a news clip of Sergeant Peters stating they had no evidence yet to support this.

Senator Leo Thompson appeared on the program. He pushed for the boys' case to be pursued and shared the story of the brutal murder of a man and child at the gorge in 1822. He also mentioned the alleged ghost sightings in the same area. Laura was elated, frustrated, and appalled at the same time. Elated that the killing of the convict, Michael, and the baby was being publicised, while at the same time frustrated that her efforts to uncover the truth had been gazumped by a television program, and appalled that Wallaby Rock's idyllic small-town reputation was forever tarnished. It led Laura to question, yet again, whether her hometown was a magnet for bad people and evil deeds.

As the search for Mia dragged on, confinement to the farm drove Laura crazy. After months of sporadic pandemic lockdowns, the last thing Laura wanted was to be stuck on the farm every day. She called or messaged Joanna every night to check on her. Each time, Joanna reassured Laura she was fine and told her not to worry.

More than a week passed and, still, no sign of Mia. Jack and Henry had taken turns helping with the operation so at least one of them could sleep and keep the farm ticking over. But as more days dragged by without any sign of the missing teenager, deep shadows appeared under their eyes.

As the pub was the only place that had accommodation in town, the police had called on the local community to house some of the cadets assigned to the search. The Murrays offered to help, and for the past week, Laura had shared her room with twenty-one-year-old Erica Martin from Cowra. Erica wasn't what Laura had expected from a female police officer. She was slim, tall, and attractive, with strawberry-blonde hair and blue eyes. She could easily be mistaken as vacuous and merely pretty, but Laura soon realised Erica was anything but that. Laura watched as Erica observed the interactions of the Murray family, sitting back and only speaking when she had something useful to contribute. Every day, Erica rose before dawn to run, exercise, and study for her final police exams. Missing her older sister, Laura enjoyed Erica's company, and the two women got on well.

Laura was lucky to grow up in a family of strong women, where she was encouraged to work the farm, but she'd been ridiculed for not acting in a way other people thought she should. Laura was impressed with Erica's resilience as she tackled, head-on, the many challenges of being a female officer in the police force. Laura could see Erica was motivated to protect the community, and her quiet courage and determination were inspiring. For the first time, Laura started to think she may have another career choice if she didn't get the marks for veterinary school.

The future was just one of the many things circulating in Laura's thoughts at night while listening to Erica's gentle snoring. Night after night, she fought to stay awake to avoid having one of her weird or scary dreams and waking her roommate. Only after Erica's farewell dinner, having consumed too much of Gran's sumptuous roast and Jeannie's cheesecake, did Laura drift off when her head hit the pillow.

***

Yogi perches at the edge of the cliff, staring at the gorge and river below. A sound, a movement in the trees catches his attention.

Turning, front legs splayed, head down, and teeth bared, a low growl rips from his chest.

From the darkness, he comes; shadows meld together giving him shape and form. Faceless, he points at her dog, who falls silent and squirms in agony.

Laura views the scene from above before the world tilts sideways and she falls, spinning and tumbling. Terrified faces come in and out of focus, screeching alongside her as she claws through the air in a desperate bid to survive. She screams as the ground looms up in front of her.

***

She woke to find Erica gently shaking her, asking if she was alright.

'I had a nightmare. That's all,' Laura said as she rearranged her sheets and pillow.

Erica squatted by the bed, her face worried. 'Do you want to talk about it?'

'No,' Laura said. 'I'm sorry. I didn't mean to wake you.'

Erica stood. 'Do you want me to get your parents?'

'No, don't wake them. I'll be fine. It was nothing but a bad dream.'

'Alright, then.' The bed springs squeaked as Erica climbed in. She turned back to Laura before switching off the bedside lamp. 'Let me know if you need anything.'

'Yep, sure.'

As Laura rolled over to face the window, a soft whine sounded somewhere outside. Yogi! By the light of the half-moon, she saw her precious dog lying in the rose garden, next to her window.

Yogi always slept on his bed on the back verandah. She'd never seen him sleep in the rose garden before. Considering her dream, it was unnerving, and it took more than an hour for her to fall asleep again.

***

The next day, for the first time in her life, Laura skipped school. Getting off the bus, she mingled with the crowd as three busloads of girls joined together, jostling their way through the main gate. Crouching down as if to tie her shoes, she slipped away when the teacher on duty was distracted. She made her way down the hill to the public library. She'd visited a few times, with Sarah, to borrow reading books and explore the library's vast collection. It also had a much faster internet connection than the farm, and Laura had wasted many hours on her phone, drawing on the library's superior Wi-Fi, when she should've been studying.

Laura found a payphone outside the library, one of the few left in the neighbourhood, and called the school, pretending to be Jeannie. She apologised for not sending an email or text to the absence hotline like she was meant to but explained to the busy receptionist that their internet connection had gone out again and they were waiting for Telstra to fix it. She told the young woman on the other end that her daughter was suffering from a bad cold, and they didn't want to risk infecting others. The call was not questioned. These days, everyone was a germaphobe. Laura felt a small stab of guilt, but she knew the small library at school wouldn't have what she was looking for.

Leaving her bag at the entrance, she took her library card, phone, wallet, notepad, and pens and made her way to the computers. After searching for a solid hour, she'd sent several pages to the library's printer and jotted down the titles of books to source from the shelves. Half an hour later, she was sitting at a desk hidden in a corner, flicking through accounts from different religions, countries, and cultures of shadow people.

They were described as supernatural entities, shades of the underworld, and as shadowy figures without faces that flickered in and out of peripheral vision. The figures were often seen in doorways or walking behind people. They were considered menacing, and many reported being paralysed – unable to move or call for help – when the figures visited them. Animals, such as cats and dogs, were often part of the stories, alerting humans to the presence of the shadow people. She read a detailed description of an exorcism conducted on a teenage girl in 1966 who'd reported being visited many times by an evil, shadowy figure. According to the account, the girl's visions stopped after the ritual was completed. It was classic boogieman stuff, and goosebumps broke out on Laura's arms.

It confirmed other people had experienced something similar to Laura. But what disturbed her the most was the number of people who'd been committed to mental-health wards for treatment after years of suffering from these visions. Laura thought about Joanna's mother and wondered if Kathleen Thompson had been haunted by her own version of a shadow man in the form of Jeremiah Pyke's ghost. Kathleen's visions had driven her mad, forcing her to take her own life. Laura was determined not to end up like that.

Chapter 21 – Mick

Mick and Dave had knocked off two large bottles of beer and opened an expensive port while talking shop.

'Not one damn clue. The dogs picked up a scent, but it went cold. She had a mobile phone, but the GPS had been turned off. The last place she checked in was school. The girl can't have disappeared without a trace.' Mick rubbed his aching neck.

Dave swirled the port so the glass caught the light from the television. All the to-ing and fro-ing, the what ifs and if onlys, were not new. The conversation was territory the two of them had traversed for days, without finding any answers. 'I don't know, Mick; we must face facts. It's been over a week. Unless she did run away from home, which by all accounts is out of character, I don't like the chances of us finding her alive.'

'But no trace, no leads, nothing?' Mick asked for the hundredth time.

'The killer is careful.' Dave tossed back the port in one gulp before topping up his glass and Mick's. 'So careful I'd wager he's done this before.'

'God damn it!' Mick exclaimed. 'How and why did he pick Mia? Had he been following her? Stalking her?'

The pair sat in frustrated silence before Mick admitted John Gordon was on the money. 'This must be linked to the Berger murder. So, what about the Thompson boys? You said the killer is careful, Dave. What if he *learned* to be more careful with each murder? The two boys, Benny and Jordy, maybe they were a spur-of-the-moment attack; he was clumsy, so he tried to make it look like an accident. Then along comes Yvette Berger. He buries her but is disturbed by someone or is otherwise unable to finish the job. What if he got smarter this time? Disposed of Mia in a different way and location?'

'Could be,' said Dave. 'At the FBI, they rely heavily on external experts – shrinks – to help them identify the character traits and behaviours of serial killers. I put in a call to my contacts, to see if they could do some analysis on the killer for me, but they said they were drowning in work themselves. I'm not sure how much help we'll get from them.'

Mick breathed in deeply before exhaling noisily. 'Are you heading back to Sydney tomorrow, Dave?'

Dave nodded. 'I have a backlog of paperwork and cases waiting for me, too. Unfortunately, this killer is not the only one out there.'

'Geez, this job drives you to drink.' Mick held out his glass.

'Let's finish this baby,' Dave said, grabbing the almost-empty bottle of port.

Chapter 22 – Gary

It seemed to Gary Wilson he'd been yearning for a sense of purpose and place for a long time. He found it in Wallaby Rock.

Gary's British-born ancestor had settled in the district in 1820. His great-great-grandfather Jeremiah Pyke was one of the first white men to set up a home, only to leave Wallaby Rock a few years later following the death of his wife and newborn child.

Gary had moved to the town a year and a half ago from Ballarat in regional Victoria, where he'd worked as a labourer with the state road authority. He travelled a lot. His job took him to small communities and towns across the state, and he'd never really put down roots. Until now.

It was his uncle who gave him the chance to start over. He hadn't seen Uncle Eddie, his father's only living relative, since he was ten. His alcoholic, deadbeat dad had left them when Gary was only three and his sister barely out of the womb. His father died in a car crash a few years later, wrapping himself around a tree. *No great loss*, thought Gary, and for a short time, his uncle had tried to help them, but then he drifted away, just like his dad.

Eighteen months ago, Eddie died. He had no wife or family, and he left Gary a rundown house on a few acres at Wallaby Rock in his will. He'd also left Gary documents and information about his family history, information that tied Gary by blood to the town.

Ironically, the house Gary inherited sat on a small part of what used to be the old Pyke farm. Eddie had gone to great lengths many years ago to buy the small ramshackle property. He'd wanted to get back a piece of their past. To Gary, his ancestral home seemed like a good place to begin anew.

Gary's house and the large shed he'd built were hidden behind a line of thick, tall poplars, but Gary always took the added step of parking his car behind the house. People in this town were nosy, and he didn't want passers-by to know his every movement. The long gravel driveway was noisy enough to alert Gary to unwanted guests. Not that he expected visitors. Although he was friendly with the men at work and chatted with locals at the pub on the rare occasion he visited the establishment, he had no desire to invite any of them into his domain. He preferred to drink alone.

Not long after moving to town, he'd visited the old part of the cemetery, finding the cracked and falling-apart headstone of Jeremiah's wife, Margaret, and their unnamed, newborn child.

Locking the door of his ute, Gary made his way to the towering gum tree that stood in the backyard. Running his fingers over the rough bark, he found the tip of a rusted, old-fashioned nail. The real estate agent had pointed it out when he'd handed over the keys, proudly telling Gary there were nails like this in trees across town, dating back to convict times, when they were used to tie up horses.

He pictured his ancestor working his farm and wondered how he'd felt when his wife and child died. Gary knew it was more than the loss of his family that pushed Jeremiah to pursue a more reckless life in the goldfields of Victoria. The old journal his uncle left him painted a picture of what life was like for Jeremiah and his family. But the recollections were more than just an interesting read; Jeremiah's journal held secrets. And if Gary was good at anything, it was keeping a secret.

The journal entries spoke of a vicious feud between Jeremiah and his neighbour, George Thompson. Gary could feel anger seeping out of the pages as Jeremiah spoke of one day getting even with George. Jeremiah talked of disciplining his wayward wife and of the convict he believed she'd fallen in love with. He'd confessed his fear that the child his wife carried may not be his.

Gary didn't blame his ancestor for taking drastic action. He would have done the same. When he fled Wallaby Rock and turned up in Victoria, Jeremiah Pyke became Jonathan Wilson. It was in the goldfields that his ancestor met his second wife, and from there, Gary could trace his direct lineage to the ex-convict and early settler.

***

Gary opened his eyes, breathing in the heavy scent of eucalyptus before striding the short distance to the house. Coated in coal dust, he kicked off his grimy work boots and turned them upside down to shake off the dust and keep out spiders. Always keen to blend in, he'd bought a popular brand of boots. It meant that when he was wearing them for after-work activities, his footprints were just like that of any one of thousands of workers around Australia. He'd taken a similar approach when buying his car. The Toyota Hilux was one of the best-selling utes in the country and very popular with farmers.

The back entrance opened into the kitchen, and he headed straight to the fridge and grabbed a beer. Peering inside, he contemplated what he could do for dinner. After downing the amber ale in three long gulps, he headed to the bathroom for a shower. He returned in a pair of clean work shorts to reheat left-over spaghetti and ponder his next move.

There was nothing remarkable about his appearance. He was average in height and weight. Dark blond hair hung just below his ears, and stubble covered his face. He had no visible tattoos and tried hard to cultivate a 'bloke next door' persona. He was, however, much stronger than he appeared. Working as a labourer in the coal mine had advantages, and he was proud of his well-defined biceps and abs. He took a moment to flex his arm to watch the muscles expand and contract.

Gary was disappointed the police were scaling back the search for the Stevens girl but pleased they had no leads and no idea what had happened to her.

On the first evening of the search, Gary had arrived early. He was confident Jack and Henry Murray would turn up to help. They'd lived in the area all their lives, knew everyone, and were described as decent blokes. At the end of the briefing, Gary had positioned himself to be in the same group as the Murrays. As they scoured the bushland, he had struck up a conversation with Jack to gain the older man's trust. From the time he had seen Laura Murray drive past him, he'd become obsessed with her. He wasn't sure why he wanted her so badly. Perhaps it was Laura's innocence and youth. Maybe it was the fact she came from a loving home – something he'd never had. Regardless, she was his new target.

He remembered a dog had jumped out of the car and sat by the gate when Laura stopped at the top of the driveway, and he'd drawn on this useful piece of information.

On the second day of the search, he wistfully told Jack he thought he would end up a sad old bachelor. Constant shiftwork in a dirty coal mine, he confided in the older man, was not a great drawcard for a girlfriend. He told Jack he was lonely and was thinking of buying a dog but was unsure about what breed to get.

Jack, who had not shared much about his family, finally chimed in and said Gary should consider a crossbreed. They were tough and made the best pets, like his granddaughter's dog. Gary asked what sort of dog Jack's granddaughter owned, and Jack told him the dog, named Yogi, was a cross-shepherd-labrador. Laura had adopted him from the shelter, and the dog was devoted to her. The animal was smart, Jack said, and very protective of his granddaughter. Chuckling, Jack recounted the time Yogi had knocked the town drunk off his pushbike as he rode too close to the farmgate. The man had been trying to coax Laura to walk home with him, and Yogi didn't like him. The man never spoke to or approached Laura again.

As he shovelled down his dinner, Gary recognised his success was becoming a problem. Because of the Stevens girl, everyone was on edge. Gary hadn't seen Laura Murray around town since the teenager had gone missing – he guessed her family was keeping her close to home. Then he had the dog to deal with. He'd never owned a pet, and although he lived on a small acreage, he didn't like animals and didn't keep any cattle or sheep. Unlike his ancestors, he had no desire to be a farmer. He could've kept renting out the house and chosen a smaller more modern place closer to work and in a more populated area, but he wanted to live in this town and this home. It was his, and he'd never had anything to call his own before.

He also loved the abundant bushland, rugged gorge, and seclusion. The open spaces and beauty of the bush were like a tonic to him after working all day in the darkness and close confines of the coal mine. Wearing his work boots, he avoided the main walking trails and practised moving with stealth through the bush. He loved the feel of the jagged sandstone walls that ran up both sides of the gorge, the warmth and distinct colours in the rock, and the way the cliff towered over the river below.

He'd heard about the Thompsons. People loved to gossip about the family. Said they were trouble. Rumours reached his ears about Arthur Thompson. Some people claimed he was a violent man who'd gone too far one night and killed his wife, Kathleen, in a fit of rage. Then there was the runabout daughter, Joanna. She was a wild child with a foul mouth and a quick temper. The two boys, Benny and Jordy, had a knack for getting into trouble, but their freakish ability to score tries made them town heroes. The twins were adored by everyone.

It had been on one of his walks in the gorge, as he leaned against the ragged rock wall that stood guard over the river, that the idea came to him. He had a chance to get even, to finish the job Jeremiah started, once and for all.

Over that long summer, he'd tracked the twins, following them as they made their way to the waterhole. They were regular visitors. Turning up at sunset, they'd wait till everyone was gone, then strip off and skinny dip in the cooling water, swinging off the rope and laughing with each other.

***

The sun was sinking behind the trees, bathing everything in a rosy, pink glow when he decided tonight was the night. Observing them from the cover of the trees as they dove into the water, laughing and teasing each other, he'd been jealous of their obvious close bond. Everyone talked about them like they were superstars, all because they happened to be alright at football. He slipped on gloves as he crept closer.

As he pulled on his clothes, one of the boys turned towards him, cocking his head to one side. Gary held his breath, his foot frozen in mid-air. The boy turned to his brother and said something Gary couldn't hear. The brothers picked up their belongings and made their way upriver. His breathing quickened as he contemplated his next move. He could let them go. There was still time to change his mind.

The brothers sauntered through the water, teasing and splashing each other. They had no idea he was there. Their 'not a care in the world' attitude irritated him. Making his decision, he soon overtook them.

Hiding behind a large boulder at the edge of the path under the bridge, he waited for his opportunity. Luck was with him. The boys stopped, staring up at the concrete pylons. They turned to face each other. 'We better move it. We've been gone too long, and Dad would kill us if he knew we were here,' one brother said to the other. Gary gripped a large rock in both hands, his heart racing.

Jumping out, he struck the first boy in the back of the head, heard the crunch of bone, and saw blood and flesh explode from the wound. The boy fell. Before his brother had time to understand what had happened, Gary swept the same rock down with great force onto the side of the other boy's skull. The minutes ticked by as he watched, transfixed, as thick blood pooled around deep wounds to their heads. He leaned over to check each brother's pulse. Dead. He'd taken them on and won. Now, they were even.

He wanted to scream his victory to the night. But he couldn't risk being seen … or heard. Gary rifled through their pockets, taking their wallets and football trading cards. He left their mobile phones with them. If he took them, he could be traced. He heard the low groan of a truck engine in the distance. Glancing up at the bridge, he wished for more time. He wanted to savour the moment, but there wasn't time, not today. He hastily repositioned the boys' arms and legs, laying them in a way he thought looked more like they might have fallen from the bridge above. Taking off his t-shirt he wrapped it around the rock he used to end their lives before he covered his tracks and melted into the night.

***

Gary opened the fridge and grabbed another beer before taking his keys off the bench and walking to his shed. Unlocking a heavy padlock and chain, he pushed the shed door aside and stepped in, locking the door behind him. Reaching out, he switched on the overhead light.

The bulb flickered to life, revealing a ride-on mower, a small kayak and paddle leaning against the wall, and power tools and fishing rods perched on a workbench. A pile of newspapers lay in one corner, and jerry cans of petrol were stacked in the other. And then there were the mattresses. Gary had tied these to the walls to muffle any sound, and the small windows on either side were blanketed by heavy, dark curtains that blocked the light and prying eyes. A tall steel cabinet stood at the back. Inside were his souvenirs. His excitement mounted as he unlocked it, picking up the passport Yvette Berger had stored in the locked glovebox of her Kombi.

From the time he'd seen her drinking at the pub with her grubby backpacker friends, he wanted her. Like he did with the boys, he used his days off and even took some leave to track Yvette's movements. It hadn't taken long to establish her routine. Every Thursday, she made the trek into Wallaby Rock to buy groceries before returning to the orchard where she lived in her Kombi. Gary had devised a clever plan.

***

He'd hidden by the side of the road until hearing the distinctive chug-a-lug of the Kombi as it struggled up the hill with Yevette behind the wheel. The sweet, young thing was headed into town for weekly supplies; like clockwork she was, and oh-so pretty.

Gary waved her down, walking to the open driver's window.

'Flat tyre, love,' he told her. 'Got a jack I can borrow? Lent mine to a friend. Bugger never gave it back.' Though already convincing enough, Gary liked a good lie and couldn't resist drawing it out. 'The boss will have my job if I'm late to work, and I need to get paid. My mum's been sick.'

'Sure, no worries,' said a sympathetic Yvette, her German accent clear. 'Where's your car?'

'Not far. I couldn't flag anyone down on the back road. I was lucky you came along.' Gary smiled.

'Hop in. I'll give you a lift,' Yvette said, smiling back at him.

As Gary directed Yvette to his vehicle, she chatted away, telling him how much she'd loved Australia and how sad she was to be going home next week.

'There she is. Parked her off the road in case I was gone for a while. Didn't want to come back to a car with no blasted wheels. This town's got a few creeps.'

'For sure!'

When Yvette chuckled, Gary felt desire surge through him like an electric current. He needed to get moving.

Yvette pointed. 'The jack's behind my seat.'

Like the gentleman he wasn't, Gary opened the driver's door and grabbed the equipment he didn't need.

'This way,' he said, letting his hand on the small of her back guide her in front of him.

The spare wheel was lying beside the right rear tyre. Gary had positioned it there to make his lie more convincing and to disguise the fact he'd only let a little air out of his 'flat' tyre.

Placing the jack under the car, he grunted as if struggling to position it where he wanted.

'Could you give me a hand?' Gary huffed, and as Yvette leaned down, he dropped the jack in exchange for a large rock. Call him sentimental; he'd used the same rock on the Thompson boys.

He jammed the rock into Yvette Berger's face, taking care not to use too much force, but he still heard the crunch of her nose breaking as she slumped to the ground. Once he'd bound and gagged her, Gary bundled her unconscious body into the backseat and covered it in a blanket, drove his car to the bitumen, and returned to cover his tracks, pouring petrol on the bloodstains. As a final precaution, he set the Kombi alight.

'Time for some fun,' he said, accelerating away from the scene.

***

He could still smell her cheap perfume. Feel her struggling beneath him. Gary groaned, teeth gritting as he put Yvette's passport down. He'd had to rush the burial of the German backpacker's battered body. Someone had been moving along the bush track, heading his way. He'd vowed he wouldn't make the same mistake again.

Gary ran his fingers over the black backpack, his thoughts turning to Mia Stevens.

Three weeks after burying Yvette in the bush, Gary noticed the teenager while driving home from work. Mia had been walking hand in hand with a young man when they stopped at her driveway and shared a kiss.

He was still on a high from Yvette Berger, and it drove him to want more. Then COVID put a stop to everything. Working for a mine was considered an essential service, so Gary was allowed to go to work each day, but when schools shut down and classes went online, his opportunity to take Mia evaporated.

As soon as school reopened, he started following the young woman. He'd noted how often she visited her friend's house after school and mapped her regular route home, which included her sneaking into the bush near her house to vape.

It was the beginning of September when he seized the chance to implement his plan. On a compulsory four-day layover, after a two-week stint of night shifts, Gary had been wandering through the gorge when something told him 'this is the moment'.

There she was. Stepping off the road, she turned towards the cover of the trees. Melding into the bush, Mia peered over her shoulder before pulling a vape from her bag.

What a naughty girl, Gary thought to himself. He would have to punish her for this, and delighted in the many ways he could imagine teaching her a lesson.

He heard her mutter something under her breath as her dress tangled on a low-hanging branch. Struggling to free herself, she revealed tanned thighs and pale pink panties. The sight almost sent him over the edge. Time to move.

Crouching against the trunk of a large gum tree not visible from the road, Mia took a long drag, tapping her foot to the beat of a song on her ear pods. A cloud of smoke and a sickly, fruity smell wafted into the air.

It just wasn't fair. She didn't stand a chance. He closed the distance between them without making a sound.

Mia struggled. She put up a good fight, scratching his arm in her desperation to escape. But he was stronger. Placing his hands over her mouth and nose, he felt her go limp. Sliding to the ground, she blacked out. Grabbing the phone from her limp hands, he turned it off and broke the SIM card in half.

He'd come prepared, just in case. Pulling a rope from a backpack, he tied her arms and legs together and taped her mouth. Lifting his t-shirt over his chest, he knotted it over her face before carrying the slim girl back to his property. He was careful, cradling her in front of him. He didn't want to leave a scent. He made it to the shed before Mia came around.

He stood to one side and watched her blink her eyes as she took in the unfamiliar surroundings. She was bound. Gagged. She was not alone.

He watched her confusion turn to fear as he knelt and cooed, 'Hello, lovely. Missing these?' He laughed as he held up her underpants. Standing, he unzipped his jeans as tears streamed down Mia's face. He took his time, drawing out each exquisite moment. Once he'd had his fun, he was more careful.

Learning from Yvette, he laid an unconscious Mia on a large plastic drop sheet used for painting, and, sticking with tradition, he ended her life with the same rock he'd used on Yvette and the brothers. He stowed her body, wrapped inside two large garbage bags weighed down with small rocks from the gorge, in the back of the ute and threw her into the still, deep water of Lake Tailer, a two-hour drive from Wallaby Rock.

Returning home, he hosed out the back of the ute, cleaned his shed with ammonia, and, at dawn, started a burn-off in the bushes along the edge of his paddocks. Sweat drenched his shirt as he battled to keep the burn under control.

Exhausted, hungry, and covered in soot and grime, he made his way back to the house when the crunch of pebbles announced a car coming up the drive.

Taking a moment, he composed himself before turning the corner to greet his visitor. Senior Constable Bob Fowler raised his eyebrows as he stepped out of the patrol car and took in Gary's dirty appearance. 'G'day, Gary. What've you been up to?'

Gary wiped the sweat off his face before responding. 'Hi, Bob. Burning off, mate. There's so much timber on the ground and the grass is so long after two years of rain that I wanted to put in some protection around the house. They're saying we're in for a long, hot summer.' Touching the dried blood on his arm, Gary continued, 'Cut myself trying to drag some logs into the fire.'

Bob nodded, holding out a photo of Mia in her high school uniform. 'Have you seen this girl? Or seen any strangers? Anything out of the ordinary in the last couple of days?'

Mia smiled up at him. She looked fresh, young, and innocent. He shook his head and stifled a genuine yawn. 'No, sorry, mate. I just finished two weeks on nights. I haven't seen anyone but the boys at the mine and my pillow.'

'If you do remember anything, give us a call.'

'Of course. Are you putting a search party together?' Gary asked.

'We have volunteers door-knocking surrounding properties, but we'll start a full-scale search this afternoon. Five o'clock in the hall. If you have the time, we could use your help.'

Gary nodded and waved to Senior Constable Fowler as he turned the patrol car around and headed back to the road. His mind was whirring.

If the coppers followed normal search procedures, they'd bring in sniffer dogs. Participating in the search presented him with the perfect excuse for his scent and bootprints to be in the vicinity. His burn-off would also put the dogs off – if they got that close. Even better, he could keep tabs on the investigation … And, assuming Henry and Jack Murray joined the search, it would give him a chance to get closer to the two men. Smiling, he thought, *Good things come to those who wait.*

Chapter 23 – Laura

December 2020

School was done, forever. To celebrate her freedom and her nineteenth birthday, Laura invited Joanna over for a barbeque. Laura, Joanna, and Sarah enjoyed a few too many beers and toasted marshmallows while they sat under the stars and talked long into the night.

Joanna and her boyfriend had split. She'd found out he'd been cheating on her with multiple girls, and in true Joanna style, she confronted him in front of his mates after footy training, telling him she wouldn't waste another moment of her time even thinking about him, but Laura could see she was hurting.

Changing the subject, Laura had Sarah and Joanna in stitches when she told them how she'd gotten some revenge on Liv Hansen. On the last day of school, the Year 12s dressed up and put on a show for the rest of the students. Liv, who told everyone she'd been named after Olivia Newton-John, was dressed as Sandy and leading a performance of 'We Go Together' from the movie *Grease*. At the beginning of the day, Laura had handed her a gift, a small box of chocolates, saying it was time they put the past behind them. Liv gave her a half-hearted hug before gobbling three of the sweets. The end-of-school performance was cut short when Liv ran off stage mid-act. Laura had inserted a laxative into each of the chocolates before rewrapping them. The last thing she saw was Liv rushing to the toilet. Even better, other students at the school who'd also suffered from Liv's mean-girl antics filmed her racing off stage and into the toilets – also capturing graphic sound effects – and shared the footage on social media, tagging it #whatgoesaroundcomesaround and #karma.

Laura and Joanna discussed the results from the state championships. Joanna had pulled out at the last minute, claiming she'd suffered an injury in training. Laura knew it was a lie but didn't push her friend. She could see Joanna's heart was no longer in it. Laura posted good times, but not her best. A feat she still was proud of, considering all she had going on and her sporadic training, but she'd missed out on making the state team and going to nationals. It didn't hurt as much as she thought it would. Fame, glory and adoration were not her priorities. She was more preoccupied with her future.

Laura was on edge, waiting to hear if she'd achieved the marks she needed to get into university, and Joanna told them she'd accepted a traineeship at the local council where her father worked and was starting her new job in January. Their time as children was over.

***

Christmas fast approached. The only dark cloud was the lack of any progress in the search for Mia Stevens. The local community had raised $50,000 as a reward for information leading to her discovery, but few people thought the teenager was still alive. Everyone, however, wanted closure for her family.

Laura stayed on the farm under the watchful eye of her mother. She had a serious case of cabin fever. Jeannie wasn't the only one being protective. The streets were quiet and empty. There were no kids playing cricket or footy long into the summer evenings.

Yogi was also acting odd. He loved roaming as much as Laura and would wag his tail whenever she went to the car or headed to the bush. In the last few weeks, however, he seemed content to stay close to home. Laura was stumped by his behaviour. In the end, she decided Yogi had gone out in sympathy with her. If she was stuck on the farm, he was too.

Laura was worried about the effect Mia's prolonged disappearance was having on Joanna and her father. She guessed it was dredging up painful memories of the disappearance and deaths of Benny and Jordy. This Christmas would be their first without the twins. The thought of Joanna and Mr Thompson spending Christmas without the cheeky, boisterous presence of the boys pulled at Laura's heart.

Later that day, she asked her parents if they could invite the Thompsons for lunch on Christmas day.

Henry smiled and said, 'What're two more people? Invite them, Laura. It'll be nice to have them here.'

Christmas at the Murrays' was always a marathon of endless food and family. Over the day, most of Grace and Jack's eleven children and their offspring would visit the farm. After lunch, Jack would play Santa, decked out in a long white beard and padded, red-and-white suit, and hand out gifts. It was a fun day filled with laughter and love. Laura wanted to share Christmas with Joanna and Mr Thompson and couldn't wait to invite them.

***

On Christmas Eve, the Murrays attended church, singing carols and smiling as the little ones acted out the nativity scene. Jeannie had to separate Sarah and Laura, who succumbed to a fit of the giggles when the doll that was baby Jesus fell out of its blanket and tumbled head-first to the floor.

Christmas day was a scorcher. By 10 am, the temperature was twenty-seven degrees Celsius and climbing. Jobs allocated, Laura was tasked with cleaning and setting up tables and chairs underneath a row of silver birch trees in the backyard. On red tablecloths, she set serviettes and cutlery while Sarah placed candles and gum tree branches decorated with tinsel and baubles. Jack and Henry hung fairy lights from the boughs of the birch trees, and the backyard was ready for the fun and festivities. Sarah placed blankets under the gum tree for Santa's visit. Meanwhile, Grace and Jeannie were cooking up a feast in the kitchen.

When they got together, the Murray family could be loud, their tales tall and their laughter as free-flowing as the beer. The Thompsons, who had accepted Laura's invitation, were engaged in the chatter around the table, with Gran making Mr Thompson laugh at her jokes and witty comments.

Joanna, sitting between Laura and her sister, talked mostly with Sarah, leaving Laura to deal with a small twinge of jealousy. After all, it was her idea to invite Joanna and her father to lunch. She sighed and then forced a smile. It was Christmas. What sort of person would she be if she ruined it by acting like a spoiled child?

After consuming a mountain of food, Laura undid the top button of her shorts. She wasn't sure she'd be able to fit in dessert. That thought lasted only until Grace and Jeannie brought out a massive pavlova, two caramel tarts, pudding, and Christmas cake. Laura tried a little of each, and Joanna chuckled, questioning if Laura would need to eat again for a week. Laura grinned, knowing that if there were any leftovers, she'd tuck into them again tomorrow.

'Ho, ho, ho!' came a booming voice as Santa – aka Jack – rounded the corner carrying a large hessian sack.

He called the children to join him on the blankets before waving Sarah, Laura, and Joanna over.

'Joanna!' Santa announced, holding a small present and smiling.

When her friend hesitated, Laura whispered, 'It's okay. Santa has a gift for you.'

Joanna accepted the present, pulling the wrapping away to uncover a small bottle of perfume.

Next was Sarah, who gave Santa a big hug and was ecstatic to receive *Live in San Francisco '16,* the latest vinyl album of Aussie band King Gizzard and the Lizard Wizard. Sarah was a huge fan; she had every album and loved listening to them on the old record player she'd inherited from Henry and Jeannie. Santa pulled another present out of his sack and called Laura forward. She pushed her way through the kids, hugged Santa, and muttered a thank you. She felt her gift and knew it was a book. She'd read Holly Jackson's first book in the *Good Girl* series, featuring teenage sleuth Pip Fitz-Amobi, and had been dropping hints for months that she wanted to read the second instalment, *Good Girl, Bad Blood.*

Santa handed out lolly bags to the kids, young and old, before telling them he had more homes to visit. The littlest Murrays squealed as they waved him goodbye.

Christmas was the one afternoon Jack and Henry had free from farm chores. The cows still needed milking, but it was an unspoken rule that Laura's uncles would take on the job so Jack and Henry could relax.

As the sun dipped behind the trees, the adults lit the candles and turned on the fairy lights. The strong smell of insect repellent filled the air as everyone lathered themselves in it to keep the flies and mosquitoes at bay. A ferocious game of euchre got underway, and good-natured accusations of cheating were thrown around as Henry, Jack, and Arthur moved to one end of the table, away from the noise. Sarah, Laura, and Joanna topped up their drinks and sat on the floor of the girls' room as Sarah played her new record. Joanna was quiet, staring at the pictures of the bands plastered on Sarah's wardrobe as they listened to the music.

Sarah's mobile rang, and she rushed to pick it up.

'Hey, Archie. Yeah, I miss you too,' Sarah gushed, and Laura motioned to the door. She and Joanna closed it behind them so Sarah could have some privacy. Archie was the guy her sister had been dating but hadn't yet told her family about. Sarah had shown Laura photos on her phone of them together. Laura knew he was in a band and that Sarah had started playing keyboards with the group. She thought it was wise of her sister to put off the family cross-examination for as long as possible.

Laura suggested they go for a walk, so they collected two beers before making their way through the loud backyard to the quiet of the paddocks.

'Are you okay, Joanna?' Laura asked as they leaned on the fence. Laura could feel herself mellowing out, the alcohol starting to take effect, and she struggled to be present, to be there for her friend. Joanna turned to Laura, her eyes wet with tears. 'Thanks for inviting us. I don't know what Dad and I would've done today. It's been nice to be with your family, but difficult too,' Joanna said, her voice soft as she sipped from the bottle.

'Yeah, I know what you mean,' Laura replied. 'I didn't want you to be on your own today.'

'My brothers always made days like this special and fun, you know?' Joanna said, tears now falling.

Laura touched her friend's arm. 'It's alright to be sad. I miss them too.'

'It won't be long till you leave me as well,' Joanna groaned. 'You'll get a great job somewhere and forget about life in this tiny, tin-pot town. Forget about me.'

Laura had failed to get the marks she needed for veterinary science, and after recovering from the disappointment, she'd called Erica and asked how to apply for the police force. She hadn't told anyone, not even Sarah, and especially not Joanna, about her new plans, but, with Erica's help, had already started the application process. In the meantime, she was applying for jobs in Goulburn in the hope she would be accepted to the force and start training there soon. Laura loved the farm but was excited about starting over where no one knew who she was or, more importantly, *what* she was, but she'd miss Joanna.

'No way. You know you've been my only real friend, for years and years.' Laura started to choke up as she thought about how important their friendship was to her. 'I'd never forget you or this place. Anyway, I'll be home for holidays and some weekends; we can always catch up then.'

The two young women cried as they hugged each other before Yogi pushed his way between them, barking for attention.

'Don't worry, Yogi. I won't forget you either,' Laura said, laughing.

Chapter 24 – Laura

Following a successful Christmas Day celebration, the Thompsons became regular visitors to the Murray farm. Grace, who was difficult to refuse, convinced Arthur to share his ancestors' stories of early settlement with the historical society. Grace was also instrumental in prodding Arthur to meet with Professor Smith.

Joanna told Laura that the historian had shared with them some of the stories he'd already collected from communities around the nation and had reinforced how important the paper could be in telling what life was really like in the early days of white settlement. Professor Smith was dedicating a significant part of his paper to the impact of colonisation on Aboriginal and Torres Strait Islander people, saying it was an important step in acknowledging and accepting what they had endured. The academic even contacted Laura to thank her for her initial research and for putting him in touch with Mr Thompson. When she hung up the phone, Laura realised how important it was to her that Mr Thompson's story was heard. She was thrilled when Joanna said how excited her father was that the paper would soon be published.

***

January 2021 rolled around, and still, the town waited for a breakthrough in the search for Mia Stevens.

The days were humid, sticky, and stormy. Laura was restless. She kept having her falling dream, except now she was joined by the convict Michael, still holding the baby, who cried out to her for help as they tumbled off the cliff together. Her great-grandmother also haunted her sleep, calling out soundless warnings. But it was the Shadow Man, who kept appearing in her doorway, night after night, that frightened her the most. Laura woke from her dreams drained and worried. Weeks earlier, she'd confided in Joanna about her ongoing night-time visions, and Joanna had suggested she keep a dream journal. Her friend believed there must be a reason for the dreams and counselled this was something Laura needed to work through on her own.

Jeannie had cautioned her not to wander the bush alone, but she was sick of listlessly roaming the house. Not being able to dive into the cooling waters of the swimming hole was driving her nuts. The muddy and snake-ringed farm dams were no substitute. Snakes were at the swimming hole too, but at least there Laura had a better chance of seeing one coming. An opportunity to sneak off came when Jeannie, Sarah, and Grace went shopping to buy supplies for Sarah ahead of her return to university.

Once the car was out of sight, Laura headed outside and called for Yogi. She wasn't sure if he'd gone with her father and grandfather to feed the cattle until he came loping to her side, tail wagging.

'Let's go for a walk,' she said.

With Yogi beside her, she trekked through paddocks toward the bush. Only as Laura moved into the shade did she realise the dog had stopped outside the trees. He was sitting still, watching her. Laura stared at him for a moment and then tapped her leg.

'C'mon, boy.'

Cocking his head to one side, he continued to stare at her, not moving. She whistled for him, patted her leg once more, and even put her hand in her pocket as if she were going to give him a treat. All elicited no reaction or movement.

Exasperated, she said, 'Stay if you want, but I'm going.' She had taken three steps when Yogi barked. Turning, hands on her hips, she glared at him. 'What is going on with you today? It's alright, Yogi. We'll be okay.' As she said this, a small seed of disquiet sprouted inside her. She thought about her dreams of the Shadow Man, Yogi, the gorge, her great-grandmother, Joanna's ancestor … and now this. Recalling the photo of Mia, Benny, and Jordy, Laura wondered if this was another sign. One she should pay attention to.

'Oh, for God's sake, now I'm being silly,' she said to herself.

Pushing the dark thoughts away, she spun on her heels and strode towards the gorge and the path to the waterhole. She heard movement behind her, and her heart skipped a beat. It was only Yogi. Laura continued to the cliff edge. She turned to face the trees behind her. The scene was eerily like her dreams.

'Stop being ridiculous,' she said to herself and once again spun around to admire the view. She sat in her favourite spot, dangling her legs over the ledge as she gazed at the jagged valley that opened before her. She closed her eyes, immersing herself in the sounds around her – the distant call of a whip bird and the warm wind shifting through the trees.

Yogi lay beside her. He had his head up, sniffing the air. Laura leaned back, placing her hand on his neck. As she stroked his fur, she could feel his muscles tense.

It was disconcerting. Whenever he lay next to her, Yogi would roll onto his back expecting a belly rub. She pulled her hand away. Concluding it was the heat that was making her and Yogi jumpy, she got to her feet, brushed off her shorts, and turned to the dog.

'I'm going for a swim, Yogi. You can stay here or join me – your choice.'

Yogi followed as she made her way to the narrow and steep path leading to the river and waterhole. After several metres, she tripped over a tree root. Grabbing hold of shrubs to steady herself, she felt Yogi tugging on her shorts, trying to drag her back up the path.

'What the hell, Yogi!' she berated, her heart pounding as she realised how close she'd come to tumbling down the dangerous track. She felt dizzy and a little sick as adrenaline flooded her system. She'd snuck out. No one knew she was here. If she'd plummeted down the cliff face, how long would it have taken for her family to find her? There was no mobile coverage in the gorge, so she couldn't call for help. Yogi continued to pull on her shorts until she reluctantly began climbing back to the top.

'Okay, you win,' she said as she reached the start of the path. 'No swim today.'

Yogi let go of her as if he understood every word she'd said. He turned and trotted back the way they'd come, his tail high in the air as if he was pleased with himself. Laura groaned and followed him through the bush and the paddocks to the back dam where Henry and Jack were working. They were covered in mud, and she could hear them calling to each other. They sounded grumpy.

'I thought you'd gone to town with your mum,' Henry grumbled, eyeing Laura with suspicion when she neared them.

'Dad, you know I hate shopping. Yogi and I thought we'd give you a hand,' Laura said.

Jack spat out mud. 'It's best if you don't; it's dirty work.'

'What are you doing?' Laura asked.

'Trying to clean the rubbish out,' Henry grunted as he lifted the end of a large log, placed a heavy chain around it, and gave the signal to Jack, who started the old Ferguson tractor and snigged the log out the water. 'Some of the cattle have been getting stuck.'

Laura perched herself on the tractor seat and chatted with her father and grandfather as they worked. It was hours before they had the dam cleared of debris. Laura sat on the wheel hub as they made their way home for lunch, Yogi trotting beside them.

Chapter 25 – Gary

Gary spotted Laura sitting at the cliff's edge. He was making his way along the riverbank when falling rocks alerted him to her presence. He heard a voice high above calling, 'Yogi.'

That was the dog's name; he was sure. Could this be the day he managed to get hold of Laura? He moved into deeper cover, away from a path that led from the cliff to the river, and waited, hoping they'd make their way to the waterhole for a swim.

His fingers caressed the Swiss army knife in his pocket. He was prepared to kill the dog.

He watched with growing excitement and anticipation as he heard more movement from the top of the cliff. Peering through the trees, he saw someone on the track. The sun reflected off long coppery hair, and Gary was sure it must be her. His pulse racing, he formulated a plan.

He was a long way from his place, but if he could take care of the dog, he was confident he could subdue Laura and get her back to the shed – a place where he was in control and could take his time enjoying her.

He heard loud scuffling. A raised voice. Laura sounded angry. Maybe she was not alone? He'd assumed she was talking to the dog. He peeked out. There she was. More rocks tumbled to the ground. The girl was slipping. Losing her footing. Struggling to make her way back up the path.

What should he do? Let her be? Follow her?

He had to be quick. The track was steep and difficult to ascend without making a sound.

His desire for her was like a drug. He needed a hit.

He had an idea. He'd pretend to be hurt and call out for help. He gazed up at the windy path. His moment of indecision had cost him. Laura and her dog were gone.

Not today, he thought. *But soon.*

Pushing bushes aside, he appeared from the shadows, eyes locked on the cliff above.

Chapter 26 – Mick

When had he ever felt so exhausted? Four months since Mia Stevens had disappeared and still no concrete leads. A sizeable monetary reward had resulted in a record number of calls to the police hotline and online referrals, with people claiming they had seen Mia as far away as Byron Bay. One nutcase had reported seeing the teenager being abducted by aliens.

With every dead end, Mick's frustration grew. He talked to Detective Dave Graham twice a week, hoping for good news, but Dave was as perplexed as Mick by the lack of progress in the cases.

With no leads, they had agreed to start running background checks on the adult men in town. The sexual assault on Yvette Berger proved it was a male they were searching for. It was possible a woman may be a part of it. A female accomplice could help to lure the victims in, or even take part in the killing, but Mick was convinced they were searching for a man.

Mick was relieved the media were losing interest – all except that pesky John Gordon. Like a dog with a bone, he never gave up, and through his relentless pursuit of the story, the man had become close to the Berger family in Germany, as well as the Stevens in Wallaby Rock. Both families now trusted the reporter, which meant he had a community connection Mick couldn't control. The veteran policeman only hoped John Gordon didn't cause any mischief or raise the hopes of the families. They were already going through hell.

Mick knew from experience that the longer investigators took, the more confident and brazen the killer would become. He felt in his heart that the murderer was inching closer to another attack, and the thought made his stomach turn.

His assistant, Julie, stood in the doorway to his office, a mug of hot coffee in hand. As she placed the brew on the desk, she narrowed her eyes at her boss.

'Mick, you look like a wreck. You've worked every day, every weekend, for months. I know you want to find the killer, but you're burned out.'

The big policeman rubbed his hand across his forehead to try to stem the headache that pounded in his temples. His wife had been saying the same. Their daughter, Claire, was starting Year 12 this year and was struggling to come to terms with the loss of her friend, Mia. He felt guilty every day for not spending more time with his family, but he was also angry about not finding the missing teenager – for not bringing the person responsible to justice. He cradled the mug, breathing in the aroma and peering at Julie over the rim of his steaming coffee.

'I can't take off now, Julie; not when Bob is about to get married and go on his honeymoon. I promise, when Bob gets back, I'll take a few days off.'

Julie smiled. 'That's what I wanted to hear. Why don't you call the boss in Sydney? Line it up now. Take a week, or more if you can. We'll cope.'

Mick grinned, knowing Julie and Shirley had been cooking this up. He could fight off one; two of them working together was a force to be reckoned with.

Picking up the phone, he called headquarters in Sydney and spoke to the deputy commissioner. He asked for a week off when Bob returned from leave.

The DC said, 'Make it two. And by the way, Mick, I'll be sending a constable out there to help – to cover the time off for Bob and you.'

Today was Wednesday. Bob was getting married on Saturday. They had a couple of days left to work on the case together.

***

On Friday afternoon, Mick and Bob were in the office working their way through a list of adult males who lived in town or on nearby properties. While Wallaby Rock was small, the list was still long. The process was time-consuming and sucked up valuable resources. They'd already investigated everyone connected to Mia or who had a prior criminal history. They had questioned and checked the background of Mia's father, Don, and her boyfriend, Matt, as well as Mia's close friends. His daughter, Claire, had even been questioned. All their efforts had turned up nothing.

To quell the continued disquiet in the community, they'd also investigated Arthur Thompson. Arthur had some brushes with the law as a young man, but despite what the town gossips said, he'd kept his nose out of trouble since his kids were born. Arthur was ruled out as a suspect.

Now it was a long slog to run background checks on everyone else. Dave had offered to help, but he and his team were squeezing it into their already busy days. Mick had the feeling time was slipping away. This could give them an important insight into someone. It could shed light on a person they'd overlooked, an individual who could be the missing link.

They prioritised those they wanted to check first, placing men aged seventy-five and over at the bottom of the list. While it was still possible an older person could be the killer, it was more likely to be a younger, stronger man, someone young women would relate to or be attracted to.

Running his finger down the list, Mick paused and then pointed to a name. 'Who's Gary Wilson? I don't think I know him.'

'He lives on a small property just out of town.' Bob had grown up in the area and knew everyone. Even though Mick had lived in Wallaby Rock for the past five years, he was not a local.

Not yet. 'Been here for over a year. Works at the coal mine. Seems to be okay. Doesn't cause any trouble, and he hasn't come up on anyone's radar.'

Mick tapped his finger over the name. 'How old is he? Does he have a wife or family?'

'Late twenties, I think. No wife or family I know of.'

Mick repeated Bob's words in his head. *'He hasn't come up on anyone's radar.'* The hairs on his neck stood up. 'Bump him up the list.'

'Any reason?' Bob asked.

'A hunch. Ask Dave to check him out,' Mick replied.

After reviewing the names on the list, Mick and Bob retired to the small kitchen at the back of the station. It was after 6 pm, and Julie had left for the day. Mick grabbed a couple of cans from the fridge, tossing one to Bob before sitting at the small kitchen table.

They didn't often drink at work. Mick liked to keep it professional. Instead, he and Shirley hosted barbeques or dinners for Bob, Julie, and their families. The get-togethers often continued late into the evening. He noticed Bob's hesitation to open his beer.

'It's okay, Bob. We're off duty, and you're now officially on leave,' Mick said as he unbuttoned and pulled off his shirt, dragging an old t-shirt on over his singlet.

'Here's to you and Michelle. Good luck for Saturday!' Mick said as they clinked cans together.

Bob grinned. 'Cheers, Mick.'

'Do you remember a young cadet by the name of Erica Martin? Helped out during the search for Mia? She'll be stationed here for a few weeks, to cover for you and then for me when I take some leave,' Mick commented.

'Martin? Oh yeah. I remember her. I'm glad you'll be taking some time off soon. You need it.'

'We both do. It's been a hell of a time,' said Mick, downing the rest of his beer in one long swig.

'I better get going. Got a lot to do before tomorrow,' Bob said, tossing his empty beer in the bin.

'Catch you at the church, mate. And don't be late!' Mick laughed.

'I think that's the bride's job, isn't it? To be a little late? So long as Michelle turns up, I'm happy.' Bob picked up his bag and strode to the door. 'And, Mick, take it easy while I'm away, okay? We'll get this guy. Don't keep beating yourself up about it. It's not good for your health.'

'Go on. Get going,' said Mick. 'Your bride awaits.'

Bob waved as he closed the door behind him.

Mick stared at the closed door, his eyes unfocused. The chair squeaked on the cheap lino as he stood, the sound echoing through the quiet kitchen. He threw his can in the bin, grabbed his bag and keys, and headed for home.

176

Chapter 27 – Laura

It was mid-January, and Laura had only a couple of weeks left at home. With Erica's help and backed by a written recommendation from Sergeant Peters, she'd started the application process to join the NSW Police and had picked up work as a receptionist in Goulburn to earn money to support her police studies and training. Her parents were surprised by her new career direction but supportive. Joanna, on the other hand, had taken a few days to warm up to the idea before accepting this was something Laura wanted to do and getting behind her.

Laura had been out shopping with her mother for clothes for her receptionist job when her grandmother met her at the door. Grace was flushed with excitement, telling her Joanna had called and wanted Laura to phone her back.

'Did she say what it was about?' Laura asked.

'She'll tell you,' Grace said, smiling.

Laura dropped her bags in her room, grabbed a drink, and headed to the lounge room to call Joanna.

'Wallaby Rock Council. This is Joanna. How can I help you?' Joanna answered.

'Hey, it's Laura. Gran said you called.'

'Oh, hey, Laura. Dad heard from that professor guy. His paper is getting published soon, and the story about the gorge will be in it.'

'Wow! How does your dad feel about it?'

'He's happy. He called Uncle Leo, and they were talking for ages.'

'That's wonderful. Let me know when it comes out. I want a copy.'

'You bet,' Joanna said. 'And, Laura, thanks. This has been good for Dad. It's given him something to focus on.'

'I'm glad it's helped,' Laura said. 'See you this weekend?'

'You bet,' Joanna said with a laugh.

Grace, who was at the sink washing up, turned to Laura as she entered the kitchen.

'What did Joanna say?' Grace asked.

'Oh, Gran, the article is getting published, with Mr Thompson's story in it. Joanna said he's happy the story will be out there. Isn't that great?'

'It is, and you should be proud of yourself. You played an important part,' Grace said with pride.

'And you helped too, Gran,' Laura said, stepping forward and embracing her grandmother.

'I'm going to let Dad and Mum know,' Laura said as she ran out of the room calling for Jeannie.

***

On Saturday morning, Laura told her mother she was driving to Joanna's so they could catch up and talk about Professor Smith's paper. Laura saw her mother open her mouth as if to protest, only to close it again before telling Laura not to be too long.

Laura grabbed the car keys and headed to the family's old Ford station wagon. She paused. Where was Yogi? She whistled for him and walked to the milking shed, calling as she went. No response. She figured Yogi must have gone with her father and grandfather in the ute, but something told her to keep searching. She walked back to the house and Yogi's dog bed on the verandah. Nothing. She strode through the yard, calling for him. As she made her way toward the back of the house, she heard a soft whimper. Yogi was lying in the rose garden under her window. Laura knew straight away something was not right. Her heart skipped a beat, and she ran to him.

'Yogi! Hey, boy. What's wrong?' Yogi's tail gave a small wag, but his eyes were red and his breathing ragged. As she knelt to hug him, she felt a spasm under her hands and she cried out for help, tears streaming down her face.

Grace, Jeannie, and Sarah ran to her, fear and confusion flashing across their faces.

'What is it?' Jeannie panted, trying to catch her breath.

'Yogi. Something's wrong. He's sick,' was all Laura could get out between heaving sobs as she held his head in her lap.

'A snake?' Sarah asked, her head swivelling back and forth searching for signs of a deadly reptile.

'I don't know,' Laura said, her voice cracking.

'I'll call the vet,' Grace said, turning and striding back to the house.

'Hurry,' Laura cried.

Sarah grabbed a blanket from Yogi's bed and placed it under his head.

Grace returned and, in a very calm voice, told them they needed to get Yogi to Dr Frank's surgery right away. As Sarah and Laura wrapped him in his blanket and carried him to the car, Jeannie started the station wagon while Grace raced inside and scribbled a note for Jack and Henry.

Sarah and Laura positioned Yogi between them on the back seat, Laura cradling his head and Sarah patting his side. They wound their windows down to give Yogi fresh air as the dog drifted in and out of consciousness.

When they arrived at the surgery, the old vet ushered them in and, after a quick examination, ruled out snake bite or parvovirus. Yogi was up to date on all his vaccinations.

'When did Yogi last eat?' Dr Frank asked while listening to Yogi's breathing.

'I fed him this morning. He ate some of his breakfast but not all of it,' Laura answered, berating herself. She should have realised something was wrong. Yogi always finished everything in his bowl.

Dr Frank addressed Laura. 'Does Yogi wander off?'

'Sometimes,' Laura said, trying to contain her growing anxiety. 'He sneaks off and nicks bread and stuff, but in the last few weeks, he's been staying home.'

'Do you keep your poisons locked away?' Dr Frank asked, turning to Grace and Jeannie.

'Yes, of course,' said Jeannie. 'We keep all our pesticides and chemicals locked in the shed.'

'The symptoms indicate poisoning,' Dr Frank said. 'He may have been baited.'

'Why would anyone bait Yogi?' Sarah asked, her voice shaky.

'Can you help him?' Grace interrupted. She was the only one who had kept her composure over the last hour.

'I'll be honest,' Dr Frank said, meeting Laura's eyes. 'He isn't in great shape. His breathing is irregular, and his pulse is weak. I need you to step outside while I try to clear whatever he has out of his system. I don't want to alarm you, but I also don't want to give you false hope. Inducing vomiting may or may not work; it depends on when he ingested the poison.'

At first, Laura refused to leave Yogi's side, until Dr Frank promised he would call them in if Yogi's condition deteriorated.

They waited for what felt like forever. Laura stared at the opposite wall, telling herself Yogi would be okay. How many times had her grandfather said Yogi was tough?

'He's going to be alright,' she kept repeating under her breath to herself.

Finally, the surgery door opened, and Dr Frank ushered them to an adjoining area where Yogi slept in a large cage with an intravenous drip providing him with vital fluids and his blanket draped across his body.

'I cleared his stomach, but he's not out of the woods – not yet. I need to keep him under close observation,' Dr Frank said as Laura and her family crowded around the enclosure. 'Go home, and I'll call if there's any change.'

With a final pat, Laura told Yogi she loved him and would see him soon. And as she left the surgery, stepping out into the late afternoon sun, Laura's gaze was drawn to the empty space at her side. A space usually occupied by her best friend.

Chapter 28 – Gary

Dawn was still four hours away, but Gary was hungry. He showered, cleaned up, and fried the leftover steak with fresh mushrooms.

'Mmm!' he moaned while slowly chewing through the exceptional piece of meat. How could any dog refuse it?

Gary chuckled to himself, knowing sleep would be a long time coming tonight. He was way too pumped, too turned on, too eager for the morning. He grabbed a beer from the fridge, strode into the lounge room, and settled on the couch in the dark. Why could he not get Laura Murray out of his head? She wasn't as pretty as the women he was usually attracted to.

He realised he was jealous of the young woman, jealous of her loving family. Something he'd never had.

Gary only had hazy memories of his alcoholic father. His mother had struggled to raise two children on her own, which brought a string of men in and out of their lives, some good, some not so good.

In his teens, living in the rough outer suburbs of Melbourne, Gary fell into bad company. He was forever dodging the police, and at fifteen was arrested for gang-related violence. The judge was sympathetic to his difficult upbringing, and he'd managed to escape juvenile detention and a criminal conviction. Instead, he was forced to undertake mandatory counselling with a social worker, to address his anger issues, and serve six months of community service, doling out meals at a homeless shelter every weekend.

At eighteen, Gary stepped up to serious assault. He'd beaten his mother's boyfriend, Alfie, with a cricket bat. The bad drunk and ex-crim deserved more given he'd spent the last five years beating up Gary, his mother, and his sister. Each time, his mum would kick Alfie out. When she let him back into their home for the sixth time, Gary decided enough was enough.

Gary's feelings toward women were complicated. In his way, he loved his mother and sister, but he also despised what he considered their weakness. His mum had been a doormat to the men in her life, one minute standing up to them, the next surrendering and using booze and drugs to cope. Worst of all was Gary's sister, who showed signs of heading down the same path with her questionable choice of men.

Gary couldn't bear seeing his mother and little sister repeat the same mistakes over and over again only to expect him to step in and save them. He'd had enough. Instead, Gary vowed to remain strong. Power was king, and Gary grew to enjoy the company of women on his terms.

Until moving to Wallaby Rock, brothels had served his insatiable needs. For him, sex was as much about domination as it was gratification. Gary had no interest in happily ever after. He didn't believe in such sentimental rubbish.

A month after he'd beaten Alfie – who had no desire to bring himself to the attention of the police – to a pulp in his mother's garage, Gary moved out of home, finding work in regional Victoria with a roadcrew before moving to Wallaby Rock a few years later.

If the cops followed normal procedure, they'd be running background checks on the men in town. He had to keep his head down and hope his past misdemeanours didn't mark him as a possible suspect.

Chapter 29 – Laura

Saturday had been an emotional whirlwind, with everyone being way too nice to Laura and making her edgy. That evening, Dr Frank called to say Yogi was awake and improving, but he'd have to stay at the surgery for a few days till he fully recovered.

On Sunday, desperate to talk to Joanna, Laura pleaded with her mother. At first, Jeannie refused to let Laura out on her own. Yogi being poisoned had rattled her. But Grace intervened, making Laura promise to be back before lunch.

***

Laura parked the car and knocked on the front door. No answer. She followed the verandah to the back of the house, thinking Joanna and Mr Thompson might be sitting out the back or even training in the back paddock, but the family's car was gone, and the curtains in the house were drawn. Returning to the front of the house, Laura decided to settle into a comfy chair on the front verandah and wait a while.

Closing her eyes, her mind drifted back to Yogi's poisoning and last night's dream in which the Shadow Man appeared at her bedroom window. From reading over her journal, Laura knew the Shadow Man's visits were happening more and more. She realised she should talk to her family, but she wanted to speak to Joanna first, to seek the counsel of a trusted friend.

With no sign of Joanna after fifteen minutes, Laura tried calling her, but the call went straight to her message bank. She asked Joanna to call her as soon as she got home.

Disappointed, Laura drove a further ten minutes into town, deciding to swing by the shops. Maybe Joanna was there and annoying Mrs Old Bag.

She passed the pub and the hair salon and pulled up outside Mrs Old Bag's. No luck.

A loud bang startled her, and glancing back, she saw smoke puff out of the exhaust of a ute parked outside the pub. Regaining her composure, she drove on for several kilometres before stopping the car once more outside Joanna's home. She'd hoped her friend had returned while she'd driven into town and back, but the car was still gone and there was no sign that anyone was around. Laura waited five more minutes before starting the station wagon and heading home.

Chapter 30 – Gary

Gary had just returned to his ute after picking up a case of beer from the pub when he saw Laura cruising along the main street in the Murrays' faded station wagon. Fumbling his keys in his excitement, he was twisting them in the ignition when a loud bang had him ducking for cover. His Hilux had backfired at the worst time. Swearing under his breath, Gary craned his head above the steering wheel and spotted Laura driving away.

Gary had studied Laura's usual routes to and from town and from the old Thompson house, which she often visited. He knew the best position to stop and wait. Opening his glovebox, he grabbed gloves and pulled his knife out of his pocket. Hiding the gear behind the beer on the front passenger seat, he could just see the taillights of the station wagon as it turned down one of the roads leading out of town. He knew it led to the Thompsons'. It looked like Laura was visiting her friend. That may give him enough time to execute his plan. All he needed was a few minutes to get ahead of her.

Figuring the young woman would have to drive home at some point, Gary disappeared down a side street to avoid the Thompon property and sped ahead to rejoin the road that led to Laura's farm. He drove for several minutes until he came to the spot – a quiet stretch of country road, devoid of houses and bordered by thick scrub on both sides. He reviewed his plan, deciding his best strategy was to appeal to the young woman's good nature.

Grabbing a tattered map from the back seat, he placed it on the dash. He'd ask for directions to the cemetery. He'd explain he was from out of town and had discovered ancestors who'd lived in the area. Plausible enough, he told himself. And a story was always more convincing if partly true.

It was time. He saw her approaching in the rear-vision mirror and stepped out of the car, waving to her to pull over.

He waited as she manoeuvred the station wagon and pulled up a short distance behind him. When she came to a stop, he called out, 'Hi, there. Could you help? I'm trying to find the old cemetery. I think I must be lost.'

Laura stayed in her car and called back, 'Head back into town and turn right at Long Gully Road.'

'Long Gully Road?' He shrugged exaggeratedly. 'I have a map here. Could you show me? Please?' When the young woman didn't move, he added, 'I've been tracing my family tree. Reckon I have ancestors who lived here. Thought I might check the cemetery. Has your family lived here long?'

'Yes,' she replied, staring hard at the map Gary was now waving in her direction.

'If you could take a quick look, I'd appreciate it. My map might be old. For the life of me, I can't see the road you mentioned.'

The young woman turned her head back towards town and then to Gary, biting at her bottom lip. He could almost see the indecision, the internal struggle, then her door creaked open, and his heart raced. The tooting of a car horn startled them both.

'Joanna!' Laura called as another vehicle pulled to a stop on the other side of the road.

'Laura! I was out at your place. Your mum told me about Yogi.' The young female driver eyed Gary. 'Everything okay here?'

'All good,' Gary said hastily as he lowered himself into the driver's seat. He needed to get the hell out of here – now. He started the car and prepared to do a U-turn, back toward town and the cemetery.

Glancing at Gary one more time, Joanna said, 'Laura, why don't I follow you home, then we can talk.'

'Is it safe? For everyone else?' Laura laughed. 'I mean, you are an unlicensed driver.'

'Ha, ha, very funny. I go for my licence in two days,' Joanna called, sneaking a peek to see if the man in the white ute had heard.

If Laura's laugh wasn't titillating enough, when Gary drove past her, she smiled at him, and it took all his self-control to keep going.

'Yeah, well, th-thanks for the tip,' he stammered out the window to her. 'I'm sure I'll find it.'

Chapter 31 – Laura

'Who was he?' a frowning Joanna asked as they leaned against their cars parked next to the Murray's farmhouse.

'Some guy wanting directions to the old cemetery.' Laura let out a long breath she hadn't realised she'd been holding.

'Laura! I reckoned you were smarter than that, talking to a strange fella out here.'

'He seemed genuinely lost,' Laura mumbled.

'I don't care. We should let your mum and dad know,' Joanna insisted.

'Please don't,' Laura begged. 'Mum didn't want to me go out on my own in the first place. She's trying, but she still treats me like a little kid. If she knew about this, she'd lock me in my room till I'm forty or force me to join a convent. Besides, what're you doing driving? Where's your dad?'

Joanna grinned. 'Dad had to do overtime today and got a lift to work. He said I could take the car if I stayed off the main roads and away from town so no one spotted me. I've been driving for ages, and like I said, I go for my licence in two days. I got your message but was driving and couldn't answer. So, are you going to tell me about Yogi?'

'Dr Frank thinks he might've been baited. I was so scared. If I hadn't seen him when I did, he would've died. He's getting better, but Dr Frank wants to keep him for a few more days.'

Laura blew her nose as tears started to fall. She felt like she'd been on an emotional rollercoaster.

The smell of fresh homemade biscuits welcomed them as they swung through the front door. Grace, Jeannie, and Sarah joined them for a cuppa, and Joanna shared with them the news that Professor Smith's paper would be published next week. Her eyes were glowing with pride, and she seemed more like her old self. Laura pushed thoughts of the Shadow Man out of her mind. She didn't want to bring her friend down.

Chapter 32 – Erica

That evening, Erica drove her rental car, a silver Hyundai hatchback, to the Murray Farm. As soon as she'd heard she'd be back in town helping Sergeant Peters while Constable Fowler was on his honeymoon, Erica had contacted the Murrays. She was keen to catch up with the family she'd connected with and to talk to Laura about the training she was about to start.

As Erica pulled up by the milking shed, Laura strode out to greet her.

'Hi, Erica. You didn't have to park over there,' Laura called.

'Hey, Laura. That's alright. Knowing your family, I think I'll need the exercise after dinner,' Erica replied, grinning and patting her tummy.

As they strolled to the house, Laura told Erica about Yogi. When she said Dr Frank was convinced Yogi had been baited, Erica was troubled. She could not fathom why someone would want to hurt a family pet, and it was obvious the incident had been distressing for Laura.

Erica stopped at the front door. 'Poison? That's serious. Why would anyone want to bait Yogi?' she asked, repeating the same question Sarah had asked Dr Frank.

Laura turned away before responding. 'I don't know, but he was pretty sick. He's not himself yet and will be on a strict diet for months. Dr Frank told us we were lucky he didn't die,' Laura said, staring at her feet. Speaking about it clearly still upset her. 'Dr Frank said he hopes Yogi can come home soon. It's not the same without him.'

Laura introduced Erica to Sarah, and the Murrays congratulated Erica on her graduation from police training.

After dinner, Erica insisted on helping with the washing up, saying it was the least she could do after such a wonderful meal. She, Sarah, and Laura carried the dirty dishes to the dishwasher, and Erica washed the pots and pans while Sarah and Laura wiped up. They could hear the television and the low murmur of conversation from the lounge room. Erica seized the chance to ask Laura, who'd been quiet during dinner, how she was feeling about the recruit training that lay ahead.

'To be honest, I'm a bit nervous,' Laura admitted. 'I mean, what if I'm not good enough? Not smart enough or not strong enough?'

'You will have some big men in the class, but don't let them intimidate you. Size isn't everything. It's how you use your strength and your brain. You're smart, Laura. Listen to your instincts. You'll be fitter and faster than most of the blokes. Don't let them push you around. Stand up for yourself, and you'll be fine. You know you can call me anytime,' Erica reassured her.

Laura nodded, staring out the window to the night.

Jack poked his head through the doorway. 'Would you like a drink, Erica?' he asked, holding up a bottle of whiskey.

'No thanks, Jack. I've got to drive, but I'll put the kettle on for a cuppa before I go.'

Jack nodded and returned to the lounge room. Sarah and Laura followed him, hurrying to get their favourite seats. Erica let the tea sit and brew in the pot before pouring a cup and joining them. She remained standing until Henry gestured to his daughters to squeeze up on the couch and make room for their guest.

'Laura told me about Yogi,' Erica said to Jack as she manoeuvred her long legs past his easy chair. 'She said someone tried to bait him. Do you have any idea who might want to hurt him?' she asked.

'No idea. Our neighbours all know Yogi, and they would never do anything like that. We can't figure it out.'

'Maybe we should consult the leaves, hey, Mum?' Henry joked as he pointed to Grace's empty cup on the side table. Erica turned to Henry, her face reflecting her confusion.

'Mum reads tea leaves,' Henry explained.

Grace nodded. 'I do, but not often. You never know what the leaves will tell you. Would you like me to read yours when you're done, Erica?'

Erica laughed. 'Thanks, Grace, but I'll pass.'

'How's the investigation into Mia Stevens going?' Jeannie enquired.

'Still going,' said Erica. Skilfully moving the conversation on, she turned to Grace, licking her lips. 'Best trifle I've ever eaten, but don't tell my mum.'

Grace smiled. 'Thank you, Erica. It's quite easy. I'll give you the recipe next time. How long are you in town? You could always stay with us, you know.'

'For a couple of months, and thank you, Grace, but as it's just me, and I'm here for a while, work is paying for a room this time.' Erica swallowed her tea and checked her watch. 'It's getting late. I'd better get moving. Thank you again for dinner. It was nice to catch up with you all.'

'Why don't you come over for lunch on the weekend? I mean, if you're not busy,' Henry said.

'Thanks, Henry. I appreciate the offer. I'll let you know what I'm up to later in the week if that's okay,' Erica said. She didn't want to commit to anything until she knew what her workload would be. Erica took her cup to the kitchen, and Laura offered to walk her to the car.

As they stepped off the porch, Laura piped up. 'Erica, can I tell you something? But it needs to stay between you and me,' she said as she twisted her hands together.

'That all depends. I don't want to betray any confidence, but if it's something serious, if you've gone nuts and broken the law, I may not have a choice,' Erica said, grinning at Laura, whom she could never imagine doing anything illegal.

'Oh no, it's nothing like that. It's …' Laura stammered, her eyes fixed on the long shadows cast by the light from the farmhouse. Erica followed her gaze. The silence stretched on as she waited for Laura to continue.

When Laura didn't speak, Erica prodded, 'Why don't you just tell me, Laura? Something is worrying you. Are you still nervous about your application or the training? Like I said, you can call me anytime to talk about it. Or is it something else? More dreams? Aren't you sleeping?'

'It's not the training, but it is about my dreams – well, sort of. Something weird happened this morning. I've been thinking about it all day, but I haven't told Mum or Dad or Sarah. I didn't want to worry them. I mean, I'm not a child anymore. I can take care of myself,' Laura mumbled.

Erica stopped by the car, leaning against the door. 'Why don't you tell me what's bothering you.' Erica wondered if Laura was having trouble with a guy, something she didn't feel comfortable talking to her parents about.

'This morning, I was driving home, and a man who was stopped by the side of the road waved me over. Asked me for directions. He said he was trying to find the old cemetery. He was looking for relatives he thought may be buried there. He wanted me to show him where the graveyard is on a map he had.' Laura paused. 'He was friendly, and he seemed lost … but I didn't get out of my car.'

'Did he scare you?' Erica asked, keeping her voice calm.

'A little. There was something not right about him. But then I thought maybe I was overreacting because of all the horrible things that've happened around here. He did appear lost, so I brushed it off. But …' Laura's voice faltered.

'But?' Erica prompted.

'This is going to sound crazy, but he reminded me of someone. The way he stood was so familiar. I've been thinking about it all day. I couldn't put it together until tonight. I think he's the man I've been dreaming of – The Shadow Man,' Laura whispered, glancing behind her as if saying his name would bring him to life.

'The Shadow Man?' Erica quizzed, puzzled by this new revelation.

'He's been stalking me. In my dreams. For a long time. The night I had the nightmare when you were here, I dreamt about him. He scares me. I am convinced he wants to hurt me. I think he's the one who poisoned Yogi. I don't know how I know. I just know.'

Laura's hands were shaking, and Erica gripped them in hers. 'He can't hurt you here, Laura. You're safe at home. But do you remember what this man looked like? What type of car he was driving?' Erica asked. She held her breath, waiting for Laura's response.

'He was a bit shorter than Dad and you, but taller than Sarah. He had blond hair and was driving a white Toyota Hilux, an older model.'

Erica's heartbeat quickened; it sounded like Laura had a good description of this man and his vehicle.

She gripped Laura's shoulder. 'Laura, do you happen to have any dash cam footage?'

'No. Our dash cam died about a year ago, and we haven't bought a new one, but my friend Joanna pulled up while the man was talking to me and we drove home together. Joanna was driving her dad's car. Oh, but she doesn't have her licence yet,' Laura blurted. 'You won't get her into trouble, will you?'

Erica reassured her, 'No, I won't. Don't worry about your friend, but please keep this to yourself for now.' Erica had no reason to doubt Laura and her story, and the connection to her dreams was dark and disturbing. Her grandfather, who'd been a respected senior officer on the force for many years, told her to always listen to her instincts, and Erica believed Laura. She needed to talk to Sergeant Peters but hesitated about calling her senior officer before she'd even officially started the job.

'Get back inside and stay close to home. Understand?' Erica said. Her tone was serious; she wanted it clear that this was no joke.

Laura nodded and waved to Erica as she started the car. Erica returned the gesture out the window and saw Laura in the rear-view mirror make her way back to the house.

Erica sat on the speed limit as she drove to the motel. The low-budget accommodation was situated on the highway about thirty kilometres north of Wallaby Rock. She parked the car around the back. The smell of stale tobacco hit her in the face as she opened the door. Plonking herself on the edge of the bed, she took a small notebook and her phone out of her handbag. Flicking through the pages, she found Mick's mobile number. Her fingers hovered over the keypad before she tossed her phone on the bed.

Erica paced back and forth, debating what to do. In the end, she decided to wait till morning, until she was part of the team. She figured calling her boss late on a Sunday night was not the best way to kick off their working relationship, and she wanted to make a good first impression.

She was too wired to sleep and couldn't get Laura's story out of her mind. Mulling over what Laura had shared about her encounter with the man by the road, Erica was filled with hot anger. Laura was a sensible young woman, and in the short time she had known her, Erica had begun to think of her as a little sister, but it sounded like Laura was lucky her friend had turned up when she did.

Erica wasn't sure what to think about Laura's dreams. Relying on psychic visions or feelings was not in the police investigation handbook. She knew she'd be ridiculed for suggesting they even consider those sources. While times had changed, Erica knew she faced an uphill battle to be considered as good as her male colleagues, but she believed in trusting in her gut and had seen for herself how frightened Laura was after one of her nightmares. Erica was convinced Laura wasn't making her dreams up; she believed they were real. The big question was whether they were the key to catching a killer.

She needed something to take the edge off. She opened the small fridge in her room and took out a tiny bottle of Tia Maria before downing it in one gulp. She climbed into bed, hoping the liqueur would help her sleep.

Chapter 33 – Laura

After her conversation with Erica, an exhausted Laura fell into her pillows, sleep soon taking her.

Dawn is breaking as Laura peeks out from behind the tree. Michael pleads for the life of the baby clutched to his chest. The newborn's cries are loud and unrelenting as Jeremiah points the musket at the young convict's head and pushes him closer to the edge.

Twigs snap as she emerges from her hiding spot. The sound alerts Jeremiah to her presence. He turns, and Laura freezes.

It's him! The man from the car.

He grins, but his smile is cold and hard, like the frost-covered, parched paddocks in winter. There is no warmth, no love on his face. He steps towards her.

Before Laura can react, everything shifts. Goes dark.

She is hiding on the floor in the back seat of a car, covered by something heavy and warm as the vehicle bounces up and down a rough track. It's pitch black, except for the beam of the headlights.

As the car slows, she lifts her head as the lights reflect off a sign: 'Lake Tailer'. The car bounces along before finally stopping.

Laura hears a door open and the crunch of footsteps. She hears someone grunting and dragging something off the roof.

Pulling the blanket back, she peers out. Light shines from a small torch on the ground, and she sees the back of a man carrying a kayak to the water's edge. She ducks down as he makes his way back to the car. This time, she hears a tailgate coming down, the rustling of plastic, and swearing as the man lifts something heavy from the back of the ute tray and lays it on the ground. Risking another peek, she sees him through the back window, the torch casting long shadows across his face.

She gasps and he hears her. Grinning, he points to her and mouths the words, 'You're next!'

Screaming echoed around the room. Sarah was shaking her. 'Laura, wake up! It's okay. You're alright.'

'I saw him. I saw his face,' Laura stuttered at her sister, who was now stroking her hair. She realised the screaming she'd heard was her own.

'Who?' Sarah asked, her face etched with concern as Henry and Jeannie rushed into the room.

'Shadow Man. He was at the gorge. He was pushing the convict and baby off the cliff. I moved. He heard me,' Laura said, gulping big breaths of air as if she had just crossed the finish line after a big race.

'He was the man from today. The man who stopped and asked me for directions.' Laura explained what happened while her confused parents and sister listened in shock.

'There's more,' Laura sobbed.

'In my dream, I saw him at Tailers Lake. He pulled something from the back of the ute. Something heavy. Then he saw me. Pointed at me. And I screamed.' Laura buried her head into Sarah's shoulder and wept while her big sister held her.

Laura was now convinced. The man in the ute was the Shadow Man.

He was the one who stalked her in her dreams. And now in real life.

He was behind the deaths at Wallaby Rock.

He'd killed Benny, Jordy, Yvette and – she felt it in her heart – Mia.

Somehow, he was also connected to the killing of Michael, the convict, and the newborn two hundred years ago. But how?

***

It had taken some time, but her father convinced Laura she should speak to the police about what had happened with the man and the car and about her dreams. Laura confided that she'd talked to Erica about the encounter, but Henry insisted she needed to make an official statement.

They arrived at the police station at nine o'clock.

Laura was ushered into a tiny interview room. As Sergeant Peters and Erica listened across the desk, Laura, in a low voice, confirmed what she'd shared with Erica the night before about her experience with the man by the side of the road. Laura detailed her dream in which the man in the ute was the Shadow Man and that he was the same man who threatened the convict and newborn at the gorge more than a century ago. Laura told them her dream had shifted to the same man driving to Lake Tailer in the middle of the night and dragging something heavy out of the back of his ute. She also shared with them her dream of Benny and Jordy being stalked, and she handed over the footy card she'd found at the waterhole.

Henry told the officers about the information Laura and Grace had uncovered about the feud between the Thompson and Pyke families and the paper by Professor Smith, which included the brutal murder at the gorge, and he reinforced that his daughter would never make something like this up.

Laura watched Sergeant Peters' face as she and her father spoke. The old cop didn't give anything away, and Laura couldn't tell whether he thought Laura was nuts and they were wasting everyone's time. Maybe he was regretting the letter of recommendation he'd written that helped her get accepted into police training.

They recorded everything, and Erica had leaned in and taken careful notes. At the end of the interview, Sergeant Peters asked Laura to confirm once more all the details she could about what the man looked like and the vehicle he was driving.

Laura fidgeted in her seat, eager to go home.

As Laura and her father rose to leave, Mick thanked them for coming in and said he would consider the information. Erica walked them to the car. 'That was brave of you, Laura, to share what you did. I know you don't like to talk about your dreams.'

Laura nodded. 'I don't know if it's of any use, but Dad convinced me it may help.'

'It may,' Erica agreed, waving as they left the station.

Chapter 34 – Gary

Gary fumed. Not only had he failed to get the girl into his car, but he'd also been seen by that damn Thompson chick. Deciding it was prudent to legitimise his plea for directions, he drove to the cemetery, parked the ute, and walked through the gates, passing shiny headstones adorned with angels and engraved with phrases like 'In loving memory' and 'Forever in our hearts'. He grunted at the wasted expense and sentimentality and wound his way to the older graves. Finding Margaret 'Maggie' Pyke's cracked and crooked gravestone wasn't hard. Her child had been buried with her. What Gary struggled to understand was the way his hands trembled while clearing leaves and dirt away from the words 'Taken too soon'.

Timing was everything, he told himself, taking a deep breath to soothe his thumping heart. That was too close. For the first time, he considered abandoning his plan to have Laura Murray. Thought about skipping town. He didn't want to, but Laura was well protected – by the dog, her family, and her friends. And she was cautious. He'd needed just five more minutes to bring down the barrier and let her kind heart and good intentions give Gary what he wanted. And he wanted her now more than ever.

Gary took a different route home from the cemetery, avoiding the Thompson house and Murray farm. His Hilux backfired and puffed grey smoke as he pulled into the drive. He'd noticed the steering felt heavier and off-balance. He wondered if he needed a wheel alignment. He'd been so busy with his scheming and plans to get Laura Murray, he'd missed the vehicle's scheduled service, and even though it was a 4WD, the road to the lake was rough to navigate. He worried he may have damaged the suspension and decided he'd better get someone to check it. Soon. He needed a working car.

After an early dinner, Gary grabbed his keys and visited the shed. As he opened his trophy cabinet, his breathing quickened. Caressing his mementos, he reminisced about how clever he had been to draw in and overpower his victims.

The still-empty top shelf angered him. Laura Murray was to be his prize catch – the best one yet – but opportunity was slipping away. He paused, took several deep breaths, and visualised Laura, pictured her face as she'd turned to smile at him. Something about her was like a drug that he craved.

After a cold shower, Gary dropped onto the bed, frustration making him toss and turn. He needed a good sleep and hoped that he would come up with a plan tomorrow.

****

When he woke on Monday morning, he had a clear plan of attack. He packed clothes, cash, hair dye, toiletries, and personal belongings in a large bag and placed it under his bed. He walked to the phone and called Macca at the garage. He asked if he could drop the Hilux in for an urgent service. The promise of a dozen beers, on top of the over-priced service, got him over the line. *If* he dropped the car in as soon as possible.

When he pulled up at the garage a short time later, Macca came out to greet him, and Gary explained about the misfiring, heavy steering, and exhaust smoke.

Macca's eyes narrowed, and his nostrils flared. 'Been mistreating her, have ye?'

'No. I've been busy. Now, can you fit it in today or not?' Gary's voice had gone up a notch, and he counted to ten in his head to stem the anger he was struggling to keep in check.

'If there's something wrong with her, I may need to keep her for a few days. You may not get her back this afternoon. You understand?' Macca said gruffly.

'But I have the evening shift today. I need to get to work,' Gary said, running his hands through his hair in exasperation.

'Best you have a backup then,' snapped Macca, snatching the keys from Gary's hand. 'If you'd taken better care of her, then you wouldn't be in this bother now, would ye?'

It was obvious to Gary this man didn't have time for anyone who didn't take care of their vehicle. Gary had heard men at work joking about the calendar of hot cars, not bikini-clad women, that hung in Macca's office. It was common knowledge Macca loved anything with a motor more than most humans. But in a small town, Gary had no choice. He had to grin and bear it.

'Go home, and I'll call you after lunch,' Macca commanded.

Fuming, Gary replied, spitting out each word, 'But … I … can't … get … home.' He had planned to hang around town until his car was ready.

'Hey, Tommy,' Macca called to his apprentice, a baby-faced eighteen-year-old who looked like he had only recently discovered a razor. 'Take the ute and give Mr Wilson a lift home, but come straight back. We have a busy day.'

Tommy drove Gary to his property in silence. Grunting his appreciation to the young apprentice, Gary stormed into his house and called his supervisor. He told him he was having car troubles but hoped to still make the evening shift. He had time to kill, so he got out the ride-on mower and gave his lawn a good clip. Then he returned to the house, turned on the idiot box, and waited for a call from Macca.

Chapter 35 – Mick

After taking Laura's statement, Mick and Erica knew they needed to corroborate her story with the only witness to the encounter with the strange man: Joanna. Then they could decide what to do next.

After finding no one at home, they made their way to the local council office, where Arthur was serving customers and Joanna was sitting with her head down, checking accounts at a desk behind him.

Mick approached the counter and asked Arthur if he could speak to his daughter in private. Arthur wanted to know why, and Mick reassured him Joanna was in no trouble and that they needed her help with a police matter.

With her father by her side, Joanna confirmed Laura's story, telling the police she'd been driving home when she'd seen Laura speaking to a man in a white Hilux, who left just after she arrived. Joanna told them Laura had been unsettled by the experience. Arthur sat close to his daughter while she gave her account of what happened and described the man and his vehicle. Mick and Erica had what they needed and thanked the Thompsons, asking them to keep their discussion to themselves for now.

Mick had one last stop to make before they returned to the station. The patrol car was due for a service.

As he pulled into Macca's garage, Mick noticed a white Toyota Hilux on the hoist, one of its tyres removed and a second wheel lying next to the vehicle. He pointed it out to Erica, who swiftly got out of the patrol car to take a closer look.

Mick called out to the man he had come to know, and call a friend, since moving to Wallaby Rock five years ago. 'Hey, Macca.'

Macca appeared from under the ute, torch in hand, to greet him. 'Hey, Mick. What can I do for ye today?' Macca asked, wiping his palms on a towel tucked into his back pocket.

'I need to book the patrol car in for its next service,' Mick said as Macca raised his eyebrows and inclined his head towards Constable Martin, who was now peering at the back of the ute.

'This is Constable Erica Martin; she's helping me for the next month while Bob is on his honeymoon and settles into married life.'

Macca nodded to Erica, who smiled politely back.

'When did this ute come in? Who owns it?' Mick asked, trying to keep his voice casual.

'Gary Wilson. He called this morning; it's well overdue for a service. He asked me to fit it in today. He has a shift tonight at the mine,' Macca said, eyeing Mick and Erica.

'What's wrong with it?' Erica asked as she crouched next to the spare tyre.

'Well, that's a good question,' Macca replied, getting animated as he talked about his favourite subject: cars.

'This girl needs a bit of TLC. Missed a couple of services, so she's running a bit rough, and I think he's taken it bush bashing because it needs a wheel alignment. But all that, I can fix. What I can't figure out is how these stains got onto the wheel strut,' Macca said as he caressed the side of the Hilux.

'What do you mean?' Mick asked.

'Well, it's an odd place to find leftover roadkill,' Macca said, 'and there's no damage like you'd normally find with a collision.'

'Do you mind if we take a look?' Mick asked.

'Sure,' Macca said. He grabbed the torch and shone it up under the car, pointing to the brown stain and smaller spots nearby.

Mick and Erica ducked under the Hilux, straining their eyes. The two officers inspected the marks for several minutes before Mick asked Macca to move the light to the spare tyre on the ground. As Mick viewed the tyre, his breath caught in his throat, and he turned to Erica.

'Constable, could you check this for me? I want your professional opinion on what you think it might be.'

Erica leaned down to inspect the spare tyre before turning to Mick, her eyes wide. Lowering her voice, she said, 'I think it is. Do you?'

'Could be,' Mick whispered back. Macca stood nearby, following the exchange between the two officers.

'Can we go into the office and see when we can book the patrol car in?' Mick asked as he led the way to Macca's shoebox of an office.

They crammed inside a tiny room piled high with papers and parts. Erica closed the door behind them.

Macca pushed a greasy carburettor to one side, and as he checked dates on a computer, Mick got straight to the point. 'Can you tell Gary Wilson you need to keep the car for a couple of days? Tell him it needs some more work or parts or something?'

'I can, but *why*, Mick? What is it?' Macca asked, concern obvious in his voice.

'I need to get someone in here to examine it, but I need to do it without any fuss, you understand? You and Tommy cannot breathe a word of this to anyone,' Mick said, glancing at the apprentice through the office window. 'It may be nothing, but we need to check it out, and do it without anyone knowing.'

'You think it's human blood, don't ye?' Macca asked, his eyes narrowing.

'Could be. But like you said, even if it is blood, it may be from an animal he has run over. It may not be human,' Mick mused. 'But then there's the blood on the spare tyre ...' Mick's voice trailed off as if he were talking to himself.

Erica jumped in. 'Please don't touch the car again. Leave it where it is. We'll get someone to check it.'

Mick leaned into the mechanic. 'Macca, this is important. Not a word, to anyone!' The intensity of his stare, he was sure, left no doubt there'd be hell to pay for anyone who let the news slip.

Chapter 36 – Gary

At lunchtime, Gary got a call from Macca. It was bad news. The Hilux's issues were more serious than he thought, and Macca was now waiting on parts from Sydney. He said he might need to keep the car for a couple of days.

Gary seethed. He started to think he should have left the car as it was. Now he was stuck. He asked Macca how much it would cost, and Macca said it would be up to an extra $200.

Gary swore at the mechanic, but what could he do? He agreed to the repairs and called his mate Johnno to ask if he could give him a lift to work that evening, and for the next couple of days. Johnno was in the same team as Gary and on the same shifts. He was willing to help, but Gary felt like luck wasn't going his way.

Chapter 37 – Erica

Erica was on a high. This was her first real assignment since graduating from police training, and here she was aiding with a murder investigation! Not many new officers were given an opportunity like this. They could be on the cusp of a much-needed breakthrough in the case, and she was determined to repay their faith in her and do a good job.

When they got back to the station, Mick invited her to sit in on his call to Detective Dave Graham in Sydney. Detective Graham was head of the Homicide Squad. Erica sat in the office as Mick summarised Laura's statement, her encounter with the man, his disturbing connection to her dreams, and, in particular, Laura's dream about the lake. Mick wrapped up by telling Dave about how they'd stumbled across the Hilux at the garage and what Macca had shown and told them. Erica could hear the scepticism in the detective's voice.

'Well, let's just put the young woman's dreams to one side for now. I mean, I don't want to rain on your parade, Mick, but it may be nothing, you know. The blood on the car may be from an animal, if it's blood at all.'

'I know,' Mick agreed, 'but Laura Murray comes from a decent family. Henry is a good man. His daughter wouldn't lie about something like this, especially when she's put an application in for the service. Why would she risk it? Besides,

Macca is a good mechanic, the best around. He knows everything about cars, and if it seems weird to him, then it's worth investigating. And, Dave, I'd like to check out the lake. I mean, it can't hurt, right?'

'I see what you mean. Ms Murray wouldn't want to be seen as a troublemaker or attention-seeker before she's even started at the academy. Hmm. I'll talk to the boss. If we can, we'll get someone to check the ute early tomorrow, and I'll see what she says about the lake,' Dave said.

'Thanks, Dave. Tell the officer to come in plain clothes, no marked cars, no uniforms. Old overalls would be perfect. I don't want to draw any attention to this.'

'We were about to start the background check on Gary Wilson you requested,' Dave said. 'I'll make sure the team focuses on him for now.'

'Thanks, Dave. I owe you one.'

'If this turns out to be the breakthrough we have been waiting for, Mick, I'll owe you one.'

Mick hung up and turned to Erica.

Excitement getting the better of her, Erica asked if they should bring Gary in for a chat.

'No, not yet. We need to see what the backgrounder shows and what forensics finds. I don't want to spook our man,' Mick replied.

'Of course. But, Sergeant –'

Mick interrupted, 'Erica, you can call me Mick. When we're on our own, I mean.'

'Mick, what if it is him? What if he gets wind of this and skips town?'

'I trust Macca. He's a good man, and he gave me his word. He and Tommy won't talk.'

'You know Gary, don't you? What do you think of him?' Erica pushed, desperate to know more.

'I don't *know* him. I've only seen him at the pub once. He keeps to himself. But something Bob said before he left stuck in my head. Told me Gary stays under the radar. Coincidentally, our killer shares the same trait. He blends in and doesn't show his true colours.' Mick rubbed his forehead and reached for a packet of aspirin. 'I'd like to be able to get a bit more of a lead on Gary.'

Erica could see how much the case was wearing her superior officer down and heard the worry in his voice over not yet having a watertight case. She had an idea about how they could get the evidence they needed to lock Gary away for a very long time.

The idea had come to her last night, and again as she was flicking through the photos of Yvette Berger and Mia Stevens. It wouldn't go away. It was like an itch she couldn't scratch. She figured she might as well put it forward. What did she have to lose?

'Okay, so what do we know? The killer likes women. Attractive, young women. He likes to hunt them, hurt them, and dominate them. What if we took the fight to him?'

'What are you getting at, Erica?' Mick asked.

'Gary Wilson doesn't know me, does he? I'm not a local,' Erica started.

'No, I don't think so. He helped on the search a couple of times, and you were also in the search party, but he was in a different group and covering different terrain. Why? What are you thinking?' Mick's voice betrayed his curiosity as to where this was going.

'You think there is a link between the twins' deaths and the other two cases, but you said Detective Graham isn't convinced because the killer is more interested in women – in particular, young women. What if we turn the tables on him and try luring him in rather than waiting for him to act?' Her words ran into each other in her excitement.

Erica held her breath as Mick considered her idea. 'What you're suggesting might work, but as I said, I want to wait and see what forensics uncover and if they find anything at the lake. We'll also have some information from the background check soon. I doubt Gary will leave without his car. Macca will let us know if he tries to pick it up. Let's discuss it again once we know if he's a genuine suspect or not.'

Deflated, Erica nodded, and Mick changed the subject. 'What are you up to this evening, Erica? Would you like to have dinner with Shirley and me?'

'Thanks, Mick, but I think I'll just grab something on my way home and have an early night.'

Around four o'clock, Dave called telling them he'd informed headquarters of the latest development and had approval for an officer to examine Gary's car. They would be there by 8 am. They also got approval for a team to scour the lake. Police divers would be there in the morning. Dave finished by telling them they'd discovered something interesting about Gary Wilson through the background check.

'First, Gary Wilson has a pretty clean record in New South Wales. A couple of speeding tickets but nothing of interest. However, we traced him back to Victoria. Gary grew up in outer Melbourne. Was the leader of a teenage gang with a pretty bad name. Most of the gang members have done, or are now doing, time. They were involved in theft and assault. Gary was fifteen the last time he got into serious trouble, but he got a sympathetic judge and was issued with official warnings, community service time, and court-enforced counselling. As he was a juvenile and escaped a conviction, he didn't come up on our first scan of locals with a record.'

'How serious was the assault?' Mick asked.

'I spoke to VICPOL, and they told me the gang beat up some kids in a rival group. A tussle over turf. It was nasty. One of the kids in the other gang ended up with a major brain injury as a result of repeated blows to the head. They also suspected him of a vicious assault on a shop owner, someone the gang had a run-in with, but they didn't have enough proof to pursue a conviction, and the shop owner refused to press charges. I did some more digging and called Victorian Community Services. I managed to track down the social worker assigned to Gary's case. She's a woman in her sixties and is about to retire. She said she dealt with hundreds of troubled kids over the last thirty years, and I didn't hold out any hope of getting anything useful, so I was surprised when she remembered him. Said she felt sorry for him because he had a rough upbringing. The counsellor called his mum a functioning junkie. When I pushed for more, she confided that Gary tended to violent outbursts in their sessions. So violent that at times he scared her.'

'So where do we go from here? Do we have enough for a search warrant? To bring him in for questioning?' Mick asked.

'If the team says the stains are human blood, and Ms Murray and Ms Thompson confirm the man in the car is Gary Wilson, then we bring him in. And, Mick, some of my men are on their way. They should be there in an hour. I won't be far behind. The boss wants us to keep an eye on our suspect. Do you think you could put us up at your place, just for tonight, till we get things sorted?'

'Of course, Dave. I'll let Shirley know. And thanks, mate. You uncovered some great intel. Erica and I will pay a visit to the Murrays and Thompsons tonight and hopefully get confirmation Gary Wilson was the man that approached Miss Murray in the car.' Erica saw Mick glance at her before continuing. 'Erica had an interesting idea. I'd like to run it past you,' he started.

'Go on.' The sound of shuffling papers suggested Dave was only part-listening.

'What if we turn the tables on him? What if we use Erica to lure him in? She is ...' Mick coughed. '... an attractive young woman. The sort of woman we think he'd be interested in, judging from his past behaviour.'

Erica blushed, but her eyes were fixed on the phone as she waited for Dave's response.

'So, try and bait him?' Dave sounded more attentive. 'Interesting. Let me think about it. We'd need approval for an operation like that. How many people know Erica is a cop?'

'Erica was here before, as a cadet – when we were searching for Mia Stevens. But she and Gary were assigned to different areas, and Gary only helped out for a couple of days. Not many people know Erica is filling in for Bob. She only started today and is staying at a motel out of town. But word gets around fast. If we were to try something, we'd have to do it soon,' Mick urged.

'Hmm. Let me talk to the boss and get his opinion. We'd need a wire and a hidden camera. In the meantime, it's best if Erica doesn't go to the pub or hang around town too much.'

'Got it,' Mick said.

'I'll get back to you as quick as I can,' Dave said. 'Good work, Mick. You too, Erica. Now, keep your heads screwed on. Do not do anything foolish. Fingers crossed we can bring this Gary Wilson in for questioning very soon.'

The phone clicked, and Mick turned to Erica. 'You said you wanted an early night, but are you up for some overtime this evening?'

Erica nodded, and they got to work.

Mick visited Macca's garage to tell him an officer would be there early in the morning to examine the car. While he was gone, Erica contacted the mine where Gary worked. Mick had told her to be careful about what she said, they didn't want word of the police sniffing around to get back to Gary and spook him.

Erica was patched through to the mine's personnel department and pretended she was from a bank where Gary was applying for a loan. She said she was conducting a reference and credit check. The woman at the personnel department lapped it up, emailing through a copy of Gary's contract and a photo from his work card to prove his identity along with the salary he was on. She told Erica that Gary's salary was higher than usual because he got paid extra for shiftwork and confirmed Gary was rostered on nights for the next fortnight.

Mick returned with a printout of a photo of a Hilux, the same make and model as Gary Wilson's and whistled when Erica showed him what she'd been sent from the mine. Then they packaged up their information, a portable video camera, and their notebooks. It was late when they finally headed out the door.

Chapter 38 – Mick

The lights were still on at the Murray farmhouse when they arrived. Mick carried a folder, with a photo of Gary Wilson and images of a Hilux like Gary's tucked inside. Henry came to the front door to greet them.

'Bit late for a social visit, Mick,' Henry said, his eyes darting between the folder Mick was holding and the bag Erica was carrying.

'Hello, Henry. I'm sorry to disturb you at this hour, but we'd like to talk to Laura. It's important.'

Henry baulked. 'She gave you a statement. Does she need to say anything more? She's pretty tired and was on her way to bed.'

Erica glanced at her superior before speaking up. 'We just need to confirm a few things, Henry. It won't take long, but it's important we get this done tonight.'

Mick saw the creases on Henry's tanned face deepen as he contemplated their request, but then he nodded and ushered them into the kitchen, telling them he'd get Laura. As he left them, Jack, Grace, and Jeannie came into the kitchen, having overheard the exchange at the front door. Mick suggested Jeannie and Henry sit in on the conversation. Jack and Grace excused themselves and returned to the lounge room, closing the door behind them.

Henry returned, leading Laura, who was in her pyjamas and slippers and looked more like an errant child than a nineteen-year-old. As she took a seat at the kitchen table, Henry and Jeannie hovered protectively behind her. Henry gripped the adjacent chair, and Jeannie grasped her daughter's shoulders. Deep shadows under Laura's blue eyes hinted at the stress she'd been under. She turned to Erica, who smiled back at her.

'Hello, Laura,' Mick began. 'We have a few more questions to ask you. Some things we need to clarify about the statement you supplied earlier today.'

'Alright,' Laura replied.

'I'd like to record you if that's okay with you?' Mick asked, and Laura nodded her consent. Erica pressed 'Record' on the small camera she'd pulled out of her bag and placed it on the table before picking up her pen and notepad ready to take down details.

'The date is Monday 18 January 2021. The time is 8.20 pm. This is Sergeant Mick Peters, Senior Officer at Wallaby Rock Police Station, interviewing Ms Laura Murray, nineteen years of age and a resident at 22 Charles Road, Wallaby Rock. Ms Murray, you provided a statement at 9.10 am on Monday 18 January 2021, where you described an encounter with a man who stopped to ask you for directions. I'll now read out your earlier statement.'

Mick recounted what Laura had told them earlier, and when he finished, he asked if she could confirm her statement was still correct, including her description of the man, his car, and that he had frightened her.

'That's correct,' Laura said. 'That's what happened.'

Mick opened the folder and pulled out a photo of Gary Wilson. It was a copy from Gary's employment card at the mine, but they'd blacked out his name and other identifying details. Mick passed the photo to Laura. 'Do you recognise this person?' The teenager studied it carefully before nodding and saying, 'Yes. That's him.'

'Are you saying this is the man who stopped you for directions? Are you one hundred per cent sure, Ms Murray?'

'Yes, I'm sure. I remember him. Joanna saw him too.'

'We'll be talking to Ms Thompson as well this evening. Constable Martin, please note for the record that Ms Murray has positively identified Mr Gary Wilson.' He turned back to Laura.

'Was this the sort of car the man was driving?' Mick asked, pushing the image in front of her.

'Yes, that's it. They're pretty popular around here. Every second person has one,' Laura said, peering at the image.

'Note Ms Murray has positively identified a 2010 white Toyota Hilux,' Mick said to the camera and Erica.

'Do you, by any chance, remember the number plate of the vehicle?' Mick pushed.

'No,' Laura confessed, 'but it was that make and model.'

'Thank you, Ms Murray. We appreciate your assistance.' Speaking to the camera, Mick confirmed the time the interview concluded, and Erica turned off the machine. Mick turned his attention back to the Murrays. 'At this stage, all I can share is that Mr Wilson is someone we are investigating. We are at a very sensitive stage in our investigation, and Laura's testimony is important. For this reason, I ask that you please do not talk to anyone, even your friend Joanna,' Mick said to Laura, 'about what we've discussed tonight. We can't jeopardise any potential official processes down the track.'

Mick stood, gathering the folder and camera into his arms. 'We have to pay a visit to Ms Thompson now, but thank you again for your time this evening.'

'Mick, before you go ... Is Laura safe? Could this man try something ... again?' Henry's voice shook, and he cleared his throat.

'Yes, she's safe. Don't worry. We are keeping a close eye on everything,' Mick said, patting Henry's back.

Their next stop was the Thompsons'. Arthur was not as welcoming as the Murrays but let them inside to interview Joanna. He sat close to his daughter while she corroborated her earlier statement and confirmed Gary Wilson was the man she'd seen and the make and model of the vehicle. Mick and Erica had what they needed and thanked the Thompsons, asking them to keep their discussion to themselves for now. They were walking to the patrol car when Arthur called out to Mick.

'You think this fella has something to do with my boys, don't you?' he asked, his voice breaking.

Mick turned to face the man who had suffered so much already. 'We don't have any evidence to confirm that … not yet Arthur. But he is a person of interest to *all* of our cases.'

Chapter 39 – Arthur

Arthur grimaced and clutched at his heart as he watched the back of the police car fade away.

He stood alone, trying to catch his breath. It felt like all the muscles across his chest were being squeezed. He felt light-headed. Dizzy.

The counsellor he'd been seeing since the boys were killed told him this was a common reaction to grief when a loved one is taken away from you. She called them panic attacks. In his mind, Arthur pictured a fault line across his heart. Every time he thought of the boys, the line got deeper. Longer. Wider. Soon, he feared, it would break in two.

He didn't know if he would ever get over losing his sons, or his wife.

His thoughts turned to Laura Murray. Laura was a good friend to his daughter and a kind soul. The Murrays were decent people. Unlike others in town, they had welcomed him and Joanna into their home. Their acceptance of his family was not what he was expecting, but then again, he didn't have a high opinion of many people.

He pictured Henry and Jeannie losing their daughter like he lost Benny and Jordy. Tears unexpectedly seeped from his eyes. He let them fall. No parent should ever have to bury their child.

He focused on his breathing. His hand across his chest, he counted the beats of his heart until they slowed. The pain started to ease. He wasn't aware that Joanna was standing next to him until she took his other hand. 'Dad, are you alright?'

Arthur dropped his hand from his chest and turned to face his daughter. He didn't need Joanna to fret any more than she already did. She was always watching him. Checking if he was eating, sleeping, or coping – taking care of him.

'I'm sorry I didn't tell you, Dad. Laura was worried her parents would go nuts.'

Arthur pulled his daughter into him and hugged her hard. Joanna was all he had left. They stood on the front verandah, holding each other for what felt like a long time, then slowly made their way inside.

Chapter 40 – Mick

On Tuesday at 6 am, nursing large mugs of coffee, Mick, Erica, and Dave squeezed into Mick's office, trying to fit the pieces of the puzzle together. Erica kept coming back to Laura's dreams and their potential connection to the killer. Mick found it interesting but didn't place a lot of credence in psychic powers.

'I'm no shrink, but you said Laura knew the Thompson boys and went to school with Mia Stevens. You also said she was upset about her dog. It could be the dreams are her subconscious trying to sort through those terrible events,' Mick concluded.

While two men from Dave's team watched Gary, Dave suggested Erica review the case files. He told Mick she may pick something up that the two of them had missed as she wasn't as familiar with the case details. Meanwhile, Mick and Dave took a call from Macca.

The Scottish mechanic let them know an officer had just arrived to look at the Hilux and shared with them Gary's frustration with the delay on his car.

'He wasn't too happy. Swore at me, he did, Mick. Almost made me blush,' Macca joked.

'Just let me know if he turns up and tries to take the car,' Mick warned.

'He isn't gonna get far with it up on the hoist.' Macca laughed, and Mick couldn't help but smile.

'Thanks, Macca. I'll talk to you later – let you know how long to keep the Hilux.' Mick hung up to find Erica hovering in the doorway. She was holding the case files.

'What is it, Erica? Have you found something?'

The young woman looked like she wasn't sure whether to share what she was mulling over, but Mick beckoned her into the office, and she closed the door behind her.

'I have found something, but I wasn't sure if I should say anything.' Erica looked at Mick and then at Dave, indecision clear on her face.

'It's alright, Erica. We want to hear what you have to say,' Mick encouraged her.

'Right, well. What is the common thread in the Thompson, Berger, and Stevens cases? This town, and for two of the cases, the gorge. I keep coming back to Laura and her dreams and how they lead back to the gorge.

'I read this article while I was researching cold cases during my cadet training. It was about a concept called Psychogeography. The article was about Jack the Ripper. Everyone knows the story. He stalked and murdered women, mostly prostitutes, in the late 1880s in Whitechapel, London, but was never caught. Back then, Whitechapel was pretty seedy. It's a lot nicer these days, but the stigma of the murders is still there. Not just in the tacky tours you can do but in the way people see the place. It's like it can't break free from what happened all those years ago. And there have been more murders, more lives taken. People talk about crazy copycat killers, but this article spoke about the place, not the people.' Erica paused, and Mick nodded for her to continue.

'The article speculated that a place holds memories of things that have happened there, like people. I know it sounds crazy, but what if there is something in this? What if the gorge is tainted? Has been since the murder of the convict and baby Laura dreamt of? Perhaps the ghosts people report seeing and odd things they hear are an echo of the past.' Erica took a deep breath, eyeing her superior officers.

Mick took a few moments to process what Erica had shared. He didn't want to crush her initiative but knew that this would never hold up. 'That's interesting, but nothing more than speculation, Erica. I can't see how we can use it. It would get thrown out of court in an instant,' he said gently. 'But I like your way of thinking; don't lose that. We need innovative approaches and fresh ideas rather than the usual pale, stale men running the show,' he joked as he nudged Dave.

***

Luke Riley, a young forensics officer, arrived at the station around 2 pm dressed in a pair of old, dirty overalls. He'd been examining Gary's car and collecting evidence all morning. He looked the part of a mechanic, and Mick was impressed. The only thing out of place was his short, neat, and well-groomed hair – hair that screamed working professional.

Mick led Luke into the small interview room where Dave was working, and Erica joined them. Julie handed them fresh coffee before leaving them alone.

'So?' Mick asked.

Luke sank into a chair and blew on his coffee before taking a long sip. 'I can't say one hundred per cent until I do the analysis back in the lab, but I would put money on the table it's blood. The larger stain and the smaller spots resemble blood spatter. The tests will tell us if it's human, and if it is, we should get some idea of how old the stains are,' Luke said. 'I also found this.' He pulled a vial out of the pocket of his overalls and handed it to Mick.

'Appears to be human. Long, blond hair,' Luke went on. 'They were buried deep in the carpet of the back seat and would have been easy to miss when cleaning and vacuuming the car,' Luke concluded.

'The owner has blond hair,' Mick said, turning the vial in his hand, 'but so did Yvette Berger and Mia Stevens.' He passed it back to Luke. 'How soon before you can confirm the blood sample?' Mick asked, trying to keep his excitement in check.

'I'm heading back to Sydney now,' Luke said. 'I'll go straight to the lab, and I won't leave tonight until I have an answer for you, but it may be late.'

Julie loaded Luke up with sandwiches and a thermos of coffee for the trip back to Sydney while Mick, Erica, and Dave dissected this important new information.

Dave sounded more hopeful, telling them he expected they would be paying a visit to Mr Wilson soon, but he insisted he and his team needed to lead the interrogation.

Mick started to believe they might have the breakthrough they'd been searching for. Drumming his fingers on the desk, he turned to Erica. 'Dave's boys need a break; can you and another one of team go and relieve them for a while? Just stay out of sight, but if Gary makes a move, twitches a muscle, we need to know.'

Erica pulled herself up to her full height before addressing her boss. 'What about the idea of using me to lure him in? If the evidence is not conclusive, it may give us what we need to put him away.'

It was Dave who responded. 'Let's get confirmation from Luke and the team in Sydney first and see if they find anything at the lake. I need to talk to headquarters. You realise, Erica, this is not a game. This guy has been very careful, very calculating. He's dangerous.'

'I know, but when I think of how close he came to hurting Laura Murray, I feel sick. I know it may not be him — we could be jumping to conclusions — but after what Laura said, and her dream, I believe he's the one.'

Erica changed into plain clothes, donned a baseball cap and left with another of Dave's troops to relieve the surveillance crew for a few hours.

'It's going to be another long night. Let's start working out how this operation could go down. I need to have a proper plan to take to the boss,' Mick said to Dave.

The pair stepped through how they were going to bring Gary into the station and the line of questioning they would take. They were expecting to get search and arrest warrants later that evening.

Their first choice was for Dave and Mick to go to the mine and bring him in for questioning while Erica and Dave's team, together with forensics officers, conducted a thorough search of his property.

The second possibility was to bring him in and have Erica involved in the interrogation. Gary had a thing for young, attractive women. They could watch how he reacted to Erica, see if his behaviour changed, and, at the very least, figured having her in the room may help to break down the suspect's barriers.

Their last choice was to keep following Gary. Make sure he didn't leave town. Then they would put a wire and camera on Erica and use her as bait. It was a high-risk strategy. Gary might remember Erica. He could get wind something was up and skip town or destroy vital evidence. If it worked, however, they might have what they needed to put him away for life.

***

At 8 pm, Mick and Dave took a call from Luke Riley. Luke told them the blood analysis proved it was human, and the pattern was consistent with blood spatter, showing the stains were from the impact of powerful force being applied. The young technician reported the hairs he'd taken from the back seat were human but that, at this stage, they couldn't identify who they belonged to. Luke said he was now running tests to see if the blood sample and hair matched the DNA of any of the victims, but he wouldn't have anything more to share until tomorrow.

'Thanks, Luke. Excellent work,' Mick said, hanging up. Turning to Dave, Mick asked, 'So, Dave, with Luke's report and Laura Murray's statement, do we have enough for a search and arrest warrant?' The senior officer who'd been living the case for months held his breath.

'It is circumstantial, but yes. We can bring him,' the lead detective said.

'Excellent. But before we do, what about Erica's idea?'

'You mean baiting him?' Dave questioned.

'You said at this stage our case isn't watertight. If he is the killer, I don't want him to slip off the hook. I've been through that before.' Mick groaned as he rubbed his hands through his hair.

'Mick, hang on. I agree the idea has merit, but he may not bite straight away or at all. He could suspect we are on to him and disappear. We could lose our strongest lead so far,' Dave cautioned.

In the end, Dave wrapped up the discussion, saying he'd run it by the deputy commissioner. Twenty minutes later, Dave and Mick were on the line to the DC in Sydney.

'This better be good, Mick. It's late, and I have a partner and dinner waiting,' Deputy Commissioner Robyn Jones grumbled. 'What's this crazy idea you have down there?'

Before he could respond, a phone rang in the background, and Dave rushed off to answer it.

'Hi, boss. We have a plan. It could give us enough evidence to lock this guy up for good, but it's risky.' Mick talked through their proposed approach, stopping to respond to questions from the DC.

'What does young Constable Martin think about all this?' the DC asked.

'Constable Martin is right now keeping an eye on our suspect, but it was her idea, boss. She's all in.'

Dave bustled into the room, interrupting the conversation.

'I just got news from the team at Lake Tailer. The divers found a body, deep in the lake, wrapped in plastic bags and weighed down with rocks. It's a female. Blonde. Caucasian with severe wounds to the head. After being submerged in the water, the features are a bit difficult to make out, but the team said the deceased resembles and is about the right age and height for Mia Stevens. We'll know more after dental records and other checks are completed.'

The DC whistled. 'Well, Ms Murray may have been right after all, but for God's sake, don't tell anyone how we got this lead. I've copped enough flak from the media, and the commissioner and police minister are always on my back about it. I want eyes on our suspect. If he so much as blinks, seems like he's getting twitchy at all, we ditch this plan and bring him in. Immediately. I want Dave and his team to lead the operation. I don't want you going rogue and doing this on your own, Mick. Tell Constable Martin there'll be no heroics. If she thinks she's in danger, she gets the hell out of there. And, Mick …' Mick winced as the DC's volume increased. 'If anything happens to Constable Martin, it'll be on your head. I'll leave you and Dave to sort out the details, and I better tell the commissioner what we're doing. If any of you are religious, then start praying. We need this to work.'

Dave and Mick worked through the details. Dave called the forensics team and asked them to bring the gear they needed for the operation. They promised to be there first thing in the morning.

When Erica returned to the station, she confirmed Gary and his mate had started their shift at the mine. Dave's crew had returned and taken over surveillance. Her eyes widened as Mick confirmed they'd found a body at the lake, a female cadaver resembling Mia Stevens. All the signs were pointing to Gary.

Mick told Erica to go home and get some rest. They had another busy day ahead. Mick, with Dave by his side, made one last stop on his way home. Together they informed Bernadette and Don Stevens that a body had been discovered at the lake. They were waiting on confirmation but suspected it could be the body of their daughter, Mia. Mick reassured them he would let them know as soon as he had more news.

They left Don and Bernadette clutching to each other, and as they walked to the car, Dave pulled Mick aside. 'Hey, mate, are you alright? That must have been tough for you.'

'It's part of the job, isn't it? Not a part I enjoy, but it's the job. I just hope we can prove it's him. Put the evil creature away for good.'

Chapter 41 – Gary

Gary hated night shifts. They were long and tedious, and they always left him feeling used up. Wrung out. They also mucked up his sleep patterns and moods. The only plus side was the money.

He rolled his eyes as he clocked off on Wednesday morning – oh joy, another drive with bloody moron Johnno. It was taking every bit of energy he had to engage in the mindless conversation to and from work. He hoped Macca had some good news about his car. Another day talking crap with this idiot and he might need to rethink his target! He smiled to himself as he climbed in beside Johnno, imagining the many ways he could end the man's life. He kept flicking through macabre scenarios the entire forty-minute commute back to his house, occasionally grunting a response or chuckling at Johnno's 'oh so obvious' jokes.

Gary unlocked the front door, kicked off his dirty boots, and left them on the verandah.

He checked his watch: 8 am. He picked up the phone and called the garage. He wanted his car back. Now.

His mood didn't improve. Macca said the parts he needed still hadn't arrived. He blamed the delays on COVID and told Gary he was chasing them, but he couldn't fix the car until the parts arrived. When Gary asked if he could take the car and bring it back, Macca insisted he could do permanent damage to the engine. Gary hung up, swearing at the phone.

He made his way to the bathroom, stripping off and dropping his dirty work clothes in the laundry tub on the way. He took a long, hot shower, pulled on a clean pair of shorts, and felt a little better. After staring inside the fridge for inspiration, he fried up the last of his eggs. If he didn't get his car back soon, he was going to run out of food. He was tired but knew sleep wouldn't come for a while.

After breakfast, he pulled on a dark t-shirt, clean socks, and his boots and headed through his paddocks to the bush. He needed a walk. Being in the gorge relaxed him and helped him think.

He made his way to the river and followed it to the waterhole. He checked for signs of people before moving out of cover and perching on a large rock at the water's edge. As he leaned back, he closed his eyes and thought of Laura Murray.

He was fast concluding that the young woman was out of reach – it was too dangerous to try again. While it seemed like he'd gotten away with talking to her, it had been a narrow escape. It was risky to push his luck.

The pursuit of Laura had kept him occupied, giving him a goal. He needed another target. Another buzz. He wallowed in visions of Yvette Berger and Mia Stevens for half an hour as the river setting supplied a rhapsodic soundtrack. At last, he stood, wiped his hands on his shorts, and disappeared through the dense bush, heading up the path to the top of the gorge, and home.

He still had a bag packed with essentials under his bed, ready for a quick getaway. He planned to head out west and pick up work on one of the big stations. He had everything he needed to leave town fast and keep going – everything except his ute.

When he got home, he pulled his bag out from under the bed and rechecked he had what he needed. As soon as he got the car back, he'd take off. He'd call in a favour from one of the old gang, they'd owed him and could get him a fake ID and help him to disappear for a while.

Taking off his shirt, he lay down but tossed and turned. His decision made; his mind was calm but he couldn't get comfortable. His back stuck to the sheets. It was hot, he was sweaty, and the light kept peeking through the curtains. It was no good. He couldn't sleep. Around eleven o'clock, he got up. As he switched on the television in the lounge room, he heard the unmistakable crunch of footsteps on his gravel driveway. Peering out the lounge room window, he saw a young woman approaching the house.

She was tall, and her long, tanned legs looked great in the tight shorts that hugged her bottom. She had nice boobs; they pressed against the pale pink button-down shirt she'd tied so it sat just below her belly button, teasingly revealing a little skin above her shorts. The breeze lifted the strawberry-blonde hair that fell to her shoulders as she surveyed the house. The sandals she wore were not suited to trekking through dusty paddocks. He rated her as top grade. Not the type you see every day around here. She was a lovely, luscious thing. He got off the couch and strode out the front door to greet his visitor.

She stopped and waved when she saw him, multi-coloured bangles jangling on her arm. 'Hi. I didn't know if anyone was home. My car has broken down, and I wondered if I could use your phone. My mobile doesn't have any coverage.'

'What's wrong with your car?' Gary asked, keeping his voice light and cheery. Peering down the long drive, he caught a glimpse of a small silver car with the bonnet up about fifty metres down the road.

'I'm not sure. I don't know much about cars,' the young woman said, eyeing off the shirtless Gary.

He noticed her checking out his muscles and thought to himself, *When one door closes, another one opens.* He exhaled, expanding his chest, and said, 'Sure. The phone's inside.'

'Thanks. You're a lifesaver. It's so hot today, and I didn't want to walk to the next house; it looks like a long way,' she said, wiping sweat from her face and shuffling her handbag from one shoulder to the other.

'You would've been walking a while,' Gary confirmed as he held the front door open for his guest.

'The phone's over there, but can I offer you a drink to cool down first? I have Coke, or maybe a beer?' he said, smiling at her as he opened the fridge.

'It's so warm; I'd kill for a beer,' she replied, playing with a small brooch in the shape of a butterfly on her shirt. 'How rude of me. I didn't introduce myself. My name's Jess.' She held out her hand, and Gary shook it.

'Gary. Pleased to meet you,' he said. Her skin was soft and warm.

They took the beers into the lounge room, and Jess sat next to him on the couch. He took it as a good sign – she was already feeling comfortable with him.

'Do you live around here? I don't think I've seen you around town?' Gary took a long swig of beer.

'No. I'm only passing through. I was up working at the Sydney music festival, and I'm on my way back to Goulburn. Been helping out backstage at the gigs, but I'm heading home for a break. I thought I'd check in on some friends that live nearby, but I must've taken a wrong turn,' Jess said. 'Then the car started playing up. Smoking and hissing. Then it died.'

'What's your friend's name?' Gary knew information was power.

'Jeannie Murray. She's an old friend of my mum. They went to school together.'

Gary stiffened at the mention of the Murrays.

'Do you know them?'

'Not really, no.' Gary kept it casual and light. 'I know Jack and Henry Murray. Don't think I've ever met Jeannie.' He chose his words with care as his mind raced with possibilities. The woman was attractive. A little too tall for his tastes, but she came across as a free spirit, probably a groupie judging by her last job, and far too trusting of a single man on his own. Too trusting of someone she didn't know.

'Do you live here all alone?' She was flirting, sipping provocatively from her can as she eyed his biceps.

'Yeah. I work in the mines. It's hard to find a girl who'll put up with my dirty clothes and constant shiftwork,' Gary grinned as he leaned in towards her. He could smell cherry lip gloss. Placing his hand on her knee, he caressed her skin as he worked his way up her leg. He could feel goosebumps breaking out as she responded to his touch. 'It does get a bit lonely, you know.'

'Mm, I'm sure it does,' she cooed. 'I'm sorry. I've been on the road for a while. Do you mind if I use your toilet?'

Gary pulled his hand off her leg, brushed her thigh with his fingers, and directed her down the hall. As she walked away, he imagined the things he could do to her. He was torn. He'd decided to leave Wallaby Rock, but then she'd strolled into his life like a gift – one he couldn't refuse. Once he had her locked in the shed, she'd be all his. He was beginning to think it would be easier than he thought to get her where he wanted.

Chapter 42 – Erica

Erica passed a bedroom with an unmade bed she assumed was Gary's and closed the toilet door behind her. She sat on the seat as she adjusted the microphone pressing against her bare skin, made sure the brooch, which held a tiny camera, was still attached, and opened her handbag to check the cuffs were there. She needed to stay alert, but she also needed him to think she trusted him. When he touched her leg, it had taken all her willpower not to fling off his hand, throw him to the ground, and arrest him.

She'd noticed the lack of any personal touches that made a house a home. There were no photographs, paintings, or even cheap souvenirs from family holidays.

She and Mick had agreed she would pretend to be a friend of the Murrays – to gauge how he would react. She had not missed the way his pupils dilated and the slight stiffening of his shoulders when she mentioned Jeannie Murray.

What surprised her was how charming he was and how he played on his good looks. It would be too easy for him to get his way. *This guy is smooth,* she thought. She needed to bring her A-game.

When she returned to the lounge room, Gary was standing up, waiting for her. He had a huge smile on his face.

'I tell you what, why don't I give you a lift to town in my car? You can talk to Macca at the garage; I reckon he'll come straight out. Otherwise, you might be waiting for ages for him to get here – he's always busy. You could even stick around for lunch? I'm sure I could rustle something up for us,' Gary said, his voice friendly and warm.

Erica knew he had no car, and she could see the excitement in his eyes. She guessed he had something in mind for her, and it didn't include champagne and flowers.

'Thanks. That would be fantastic. I hope this Macca doesn't charge too much. I'm not flush with cash,' she said.

'I'll have a word with him. I'm sure he can help out a *pretty* woman like you,' Gary said.

Erica tucked a strand of hair behind her ear and smiled back at him.

Gary picked up his keys from the bench, and she followed him outside to the shed. 'The car's in there,' he said, gesturing to the large building in front of them.

Adrenaline flooded Erica as she mentally revisited her hand-to-hand combat training. She'd laid out men bigger and stronger than Gary, but that had been training. This was real life, and she hadn't come up against someone whose sole intent was to hurt her. She followed a few steps behind and hoped to God the wire was working. She knew Mick and Dave were listening in from a van around the corner and also knew armed officers lay hidden behind water tanks on Gary's property less than fifty metres away. They had moved into place while Gary was out walking. She couldn't help glancing toward the tanks as she approached the shed door.

The first thing she noticed was the heavy-duty lock and chain. It would take a hell of a lot of effort and a long time to break in. Gary unlocked the padlock and laid the chain over the handle, holding the door to one side for her to go in ahead of him. It was dark. She couldn't see anything inside.

'Ladies first,' Gary said, waving her in. She hesitated for a moment and then stepped through. Gary closed the door behind them. She heard the lock click into place. Darkness fell.

'It's a bit dark. Don't you have a light?' Her muscles tensed as she readied herself for what she expected to come next. She sensed him standing behind her and felt his breath on her neck. She resisted the temptation to take him down. She needed to wait for the right moment, to capture him on tape. She needed to be patient.

Gary edged her forward. 'The bulb's gone. Don't worry. I know my way around.'

It all happened in a split second. One moment he was at her back, nudging her along, and the next, his hands were around her throat, nose, and mouth. His voice echoed around the shed as he spoke to her. 'You can scream. You can try and fight, sweetheart, but it won't do you any good. It never does. But if you please me, I might make it quick.'

For a moment, the speed of his attack paralysed her. Then her training kicked in. Using all her power, she drove her elbow into his sternum. She heard a harsh intake of breath, and his hold on her face loosened. Dots were starting to appear in front of her eyes, and it was getting hard to breathe, but she swept her right leg around and unbalanced him. Ducking down, she used his weight against him, flipping him over her and onto the ground.

Gary lay on his back, staring up at her. He was gasping for air. She'd winded him. In one swift motion, Erica pulled handcuffs out of her handbag and rolled him over onto his stomach. She knelt, pressing her legs hard into his back as she cuffed his hands behind him.

Banging on the shed door and loud yells of 'Open up, Police' reverberated around them.

'Gary Wilson, you are under arrest for suspicion of murder,' Erica said as she snatched the shed keys from his hands and shoved him along the ground in front of her. 'Don't even think about running. We have officers everywhere.' Her voice was ice-cold.

Placing one foot hard on Gary's back to make sure he didn't move, Erica unlocked the door, opening it a few centimetres at a time. Light streamed in, momentarily blinding her. 'It's okay. I have him,' she said to three armed and vested officers crowded at the door. Erica pushed the door open all the way, and the three men pulled Gary up, walking him to where Sergeant Peters and Detective Graham were waiting.

Erica stepped out into the fresh air. Now it was over, she could feel herself starting to shake. It was Mick who reached her first. 'Great job, Erica,' he said, beaming at her. 'You did brilliantly. We got it all on tape, him saying he was going to hurt you. My guess is he's going inside for a long time.' Erica nodded and tried to stop her hands from trembling. 'C'mon. Let's get you back to the station. Julie will make you a cuppa, and you can take a break,' Mick said as he patted her arm.

'No,' said Erica, pulling herself together. 'I want to know what he's been hiding.' She jerked her head back towards the shed. 'He couldn't wait to get me in there.'

'Alright,' Mick said, 'but first you should have a break. Luke Reilly and his team are preparing to go in. They'll let us know what they find.'

Erica handed over Gary's keys. 'They might want these.'

Mick escorted her to the back porch, and she sat, relieved that her wobbly legs no longer had to hold her up.

She watched as Gary yelled profanities and pushed hard against the officers flanking him. They had trouble keeping him quiet as they bundled him into an unmarked car. Dave stepped into the driver's seat as Mick tried once more to convince her to go home.

'I want to be here. To see what they find. Honestly, Mick, I'm okay,' Erica repeated.

'Alright, but the boys can take you home anytime,' Mick said. Erica nodded and Mick strode back to the car where Gary sat wedged between two officers. They were still having trouble restraining him.

As the patrol car drove away, Gary turned his head and grinned at her. He puckered his lips and kissed the air. She held her head high and didn't flinch. She waited until the car was out of sight before letting out a long, ragged breath. This was not the time to fall apart, she told herself. They still had work to do. Rising, her legs steady, she returned to her colleagues.

Gloved up and carrying evidence bags, they started in the shed. Flicking on the light, they saw the old mattresses attached to the walls, a neat stack of jerry cans, a small kayak and paddle, the ride-on mower, a tin of pesticide, old newspapers, a circular saw, and other power tools. And at the back of the shed stood a tall steel cabinet. The constant clicking of a camera reverberated in the silence as she and Luke strode to the cabinet. Luke glanced at her before unlocking it.

What she saw reminded the young police officer of a David Attenborough documentary about bowerbirds. In the documentary, the birds took immense pride in displaying the treasures they'd collected – seeds, flowers, pebbles – to attract a mate. They jealously guarded their collection against other birds and would go nuts if one thing was out of place.

Gary's collection was more morbid.

Without realising she was doing it, Erica catalogued the items in front of her. Black Billabong backpack, high school uniform, ear pods – Mia Stevens. Passport, handbag, and women's clothing – Yvette Berger. Footy trading cards and two wallets – the Thompson boys? She noticed the top shelf was empty. Had Gary been keeping the space for his next victim? She felt bile rising in her throat and rushed outside to throw up.

***

The search of the shed, house, and property continued late into the evening with police lights set up to illuminate the crime scene. In addition to the objects in the shed, they'd discovered Gary's bag under his bed stuffed with cash, clothing, and hair dye, and hidden in the back of his wardrobe were documents tracing his family tree to Jeremiah Pyke and Wallaby Rock. DNA test results came in from Sydney. The hairs and bloodstains were a match for Yvette Berger. The news started to spread like wildfire through the town. Police had raided Gary Wilson's property. They had taken him in for questioning.

***

An hour after leaving Gary's property, Mick called Erica back to the station telling her he needed her help with the families. When she reiterated once more that she was fine, Mick asked her to visit the Stevens and Thompson residences as soon as possible to let the families know they had taken a suspect in for questioning. Mick was about to call Yvette's parents in Germany. It wouldn't do for them to find out from the media. Mick also asked Erica to visit the Murrays and update them on the investigation. The rumour mill was in overdrive, and most people would soon know who had been arrested, but until Gary was charged, they had to be careful about how much they revealed to the families and the broader community. They didn't want to jeopardise a potential prosecution.

Erica visited Bernadette and Don Stevens at home to update them on the investigation. Bernadette dissolved into tears when Erica said they'd taken a man into custody and that he was currently being questioned. Erica noticed a family photo on the mantelpiece. Bernadette and Don with Mia, their only child, in the middle. It looked like they'd been camping. There was a tent and water in the background. It hit her that Mia would never come home. The family would never holiday together again.

No one was home at the Thompsons', so Erica drove to the council office where Arthur and Joanna were serving customers. Erica pointed out the back, and Arthur handed over to a coworker before leading her and Joanna to a private office. Erica informed them they had taken a man in for questioning. Arthur asked her outright if it was Gary Wilson.

'I'm sorry, Mr Thompson. I can't confirm who it is, not yet, but we wanted you to know we are questioning this man about the deaths of Benny and Jordy.'

Erica saw Arthur clutch his chest as Joanna put her head in her hands. 'We'll know more soon, but we wanted you to know, before it gets out to the media,' Erica explained, her voice soft and low.

Chapter 43 – Laura

Laura and Sarah spent the morning helping Henry and Jack with milking and chores. Laura kept staring off into space until Sarah's voice or touch brought her back to the present.

Laura couldn't get the image of Gary as the Shadow Man out of her mind and jumped at the slightest sound. To make things worse, Yogi was still at Dr Frank's, so she didn't have him to cuddle or talk to. She felt wound up, like a metal coil ready to spring.

Through it all, she felt a pull to the gorge. The place calmed her almost as much as Yogi did, but she couldn't leave the farm, not with everything going on. In her heart, she questioned her compulsion to visit a place that was the scene of so much distress and sadness. She wondered, not for the first time, if she was a bad person, or if she was starting to become unhinged, like Joanna's mum.

Around one o'clock, they returned to the house for lunch. Jeannie and Grace were setting the table. There was no chatter between the older women, and the radio and television were off.

As Laura made herself a sandwich, Jeannie broke the protracted silence.

'I was listening to the radio before. A man has been arrested, and the police are questioning him about the Yvette Berger and Mia Stevens cases.'

Bread and peanut butter stuck in Laura's throat; she swallowed hard to push it down as Jeannie continued. 'The police are holding a press conference at three o'clock.'

Laura's shoulders slumped. 'Is it him?' she asked. She noticed Sarah's head swivelling from side to side as she tried to keep track of the conversation, like a spectator at a tennis match.

'I assume so, Laura, but they haven't released his name yet,' Jeannie replied.

Laura stared at her half-eaten sandwich and pushed the plate away. Her appetite had deserted her. She registered the sound of a chair dragging across the floor before Sarah pulled her into a tight embrace.

'Oh, God, Laura. My little sister …' Sarah's voice trembled as she held Laura to her.

Tears spilled down Laura's cheeks; she couldn't hold them in any longer.

Without a word, Jeannie, Henry, Jack, and Grace joined Sarah, lifting Laura out of her seat and into the centre of a group hug.

A knock at the door interrupted the family bonding. Erica joined them in the kitchen, waving away Grace's offer of a cup of tea and a sandwich.

'We wanted you to know that we have taken a man in for questioning. Laura, what you shared, everything you told us, has been a big boost to our investigation,' Erica reassured the young woman.

'Mum told me it was on the radio. Is it him? Did he kill all those people?' Laura's voice shook.

'I can't say too much, Laura, but he is a person of interest,' Erica replied. 'I just wanted to check on you and let you know what's happening.'

***

A short time later, the Murrays sat together in the living room watching the live press conference. Jack couldn't help swearing when Sergeant Peters said they had taken a local man in for questioning and that they had discovered a woman's body at Lake Tailer and were running DNA checks to confirm the identity of the deceased.

Henry gave Laura a small glass of whiskey before bed. He told her it would help her sleep. She pulled on her pyjamas and climbed into bed. As she stared out the window at the rose garden, she thought of Yogi and sniffed. Sarah climbed in beside her, wrapping Laura in her arms.

Exhaustion, whiskey, and her sister's warm embrace did the trick, and Laura drifted off.

Chapter 44 – Arthur

Gary Wilson's Sydney trial was a major media event covered by every outlet in the country. While Arthur temporarily moved to Sydney for the duration of the trial, Joanna stayed with the Murrays. Joanna and Laura were waiting to be called to testify, and Arthur didn't want his daughter to be on her own. He knew she would be safe and cared for at the Murrays'. It was a difficult time for both of them, but it was better this way.

Laura was struggling with the media attention around the trial and returned home from police training whenever she had the chance, which also allowed her and Joanna to catch up.

When the prosecution informed the court that Gary's ancestor was Jeremiah Pyke, Arthur's heart skipped a beat. Joanna had told him about Laura's dream of seeing Gary Wilson push the baby and convict off the cliff two hundred years ago, but he hadn't believed it.

The prosecution claimed Gary had returned to the town to claim his inheritance and referred to documents discovered in Gary's home that tied him to the area. They read from Jeremiah Pyke's diary and tried to paint a picture of a deranged young man intent on getting revenge for his ancestor before the judge ruled the journal and information as irrelevant and the prosecution's approach out of order.

Arthur sat stony-faced in the courtroom as the defence lawyers tried to convince the jury Gary was not responsible for the deaths of Benny and Jordy. They claimed the boys' deaths had been a tragic accident and Gary had found their wallets and trading cards in the bush while out walking.

The trial ran for two months, and after long deliberation, the jury found Gary guilty of the murders of Benny and Jordy Thompson, Yvette Berger, and Mia Stevens. Gary was given a life sentence for each count of murder, without the possibility of parole.

Under leaden skies, the three families stood outside the courthouse following the jury's verdict. Arthur stood at the back, unwilling to be in the spotlight. He listened as Don Stevens spoke to the media on behalf of the families. Don told the reporters they welcomed the verdict, claiming justice was done, but reinforced nothing would ever heal the deep loss they felt every day without their children in their lives.

Cameras continued to greedily swivel, zooming in on the faces of the distraught families, as Arthur quietly shuffled to one side, avoiding the attention of the journalists. He saw Mick exit the courthouse and moved over to him. As the heavens opened and rain streamed down, they took refuge around the side of the old sandstone building, away from the media frenzy.

'Well, mate, justice is done, hey. Thank God that evil monster is going away for life,' Mick said as he patted Arthur's arm. Clearing his throat, Mick continued, 'Arthur. I just want to say I'm sorry – truly sorry – for everything.'

In the distance and over the low rumble of thunder, Arthur heard a magpie call. Its song was beautiful but haunting, and Arthur winced as he felt the chasm across his heart break open once more.

'Nothing will ever bring them back,' Arthur said as he turned and walked away, letting the rain wash over him.

Chapter 45 – Laura

February 2023

'That poor woman,' Laura said as she and her partner, Senior Constable Andy Roberts, climbed into the patrol car.

'Who? The mum or the missing woman?' Andy asked in a voice that told Laura she was about to get another lecture about 'toughening up' if she was going to make it in the force.

'Both. But the mum … She's so distraught. I really feel for her,' Laura said, looking out the window to avoid facing her senior officer.

'Yeah, it's not nice, but most of the time 'missing people' choose to go missing. The rest … Well, that's not such a good statistic. These are the sort of house calls you have to get used to if you want to stick it out,' Andy reminded her.

There it was – that patronising undertone. It made Laura more determined than ever to prove him wrong. She turned back to re-engage in the conversation. 'I know that, but I don't think Ally is coming home, do you? Her boyfriend has a solid alibi, and they had a happy relationship. As usual, she was on her way home on the train, from a job she loved. There's been no activity on her bank accounts, and the family has had no contact with her at all. She had a good life, a happy life. Why would she leave it? It doesn't make sense,' Laura said.

'Maybe she had another bloke on the side, and they've taken off. Who knows! But the last time she was seen, she was getting off the train at her usual stop, only a few blocks from home. And if you're asking me do I think something has happened to her? Yeah, I do,' Andy confided.

'So, we have their statements and photos of Ally. What now? Do we issue a missing person alert? Talk to the rail authority to see if we can get any CCTV footage from the train and station?' Laura asked as Andy pulled in and parked in front of the blue 'Police' sign.

'Yes, we get the ball rolling. I'll walk you through how we do it,' Andy said as they made their way inside. Laura didn't bother to tell him she'd been trained in how to put out a missing person bulletin and was quite capable of calling the rail authority. It was easier to just roll with it.

'Murray, get in here,' Sergeant Woods shouted from his office.

Laura shuffled her way into the crowded room occupied by the station's officer in charge and closed the door behind her.

'You had some calls while you were out,' the paunchy, greying older man grunted as he handed slips of paper over the desk. 'One of them is from the dog squad,' he said, and Laura almost dropped the paper on the ground. She'd applied to the squad as soon as she passed basic training and was assigned to a station. Last week, she'd had an interview, and afterwards, they'd observed her as she took one of the squad's canines through basic obedience commands.

'Thanks, boss,' Laura said. 'Is that all?'

'No. Sit down, Murray.' The senior officer's voice was unusually quiet, and Laura wondered where this was going. His normal mode of communication was yelling.

Laura lowered herself into the chair opposite the older policeman, and Sergeant Woods leaned forward. 'I just got a call from Sergeant Peters at Wallaby Rock. He wanted you to know that Gary Wilson, aka the Bush Basher, just passed away in Long Bay Gaol. Got into a fight with another inmate; came off second best.'

Laura gripped the sides of the chair. She hadn't talked about Gary since the trial a year ago. Had tried to put it behind her. Only a few people in the force knew about her connection to the killer, including her current boss, and Laura wanted to keep it that way.

'Are you alright, Murray?' Sergeant Woods prompted as Laura sat unmoving in the chair.

She couldn't get emotional, not here, not at work.

'I'm okay, Sarge. At least he can never hurt anyone again.' Laura was proud that her voice sounded steady. Standing, she grasped the papers in her hand. 'I might just return these calls if that's okay?'

'Sure. Then back to it, alright?'

'I won't take long,' Laura replied as she stepped out of the office and manoeuvred her way to a small desk jammed in a corner, surrounded by filing cabinets and piles of paper.

She sat and stared at the messages in her hands. The excitement of potentially being accepted for a role she'd decided was perfect for her was tempered by memories of Gary Wilson, memories she'd tried hard to relegate to the deep recesses of her mind. She figured that's why Joanna had called. She must have heard, or been informed, that the man who killed her brothers was dead.

She pushed that to one side for now, and her hands started to shake as she dialled the number for the role she believed was perfect for her.

'Dog Squad. Sergeant Tyler speaking,' the male voice on the other end said.

'Sergeant Tyler, this is Constable Laura Murray,' she replied, trying hard to keep her excitement in check.

'Ah, Constable Murray, Laura. Thanks for calling back. I'm pleased to let you know you made the training squad for general-purpose dog handlers. Congratulations.'

'I did? That's fantastic. Thank you so much,' Laura gushed.

'I have to tell you that it's very unusual for a new graduate to get a chance like this, but your interview and the way you interacted with the dogs got you over the line. Training starts in a month, but I have to warn you, not everyone makes it through. If you do, you'll be assigned a permanent canine and attached to a dog squad. If you don't, you return to your current station. I've already alerted Sergeant Woods. He spoke highly of you, by the way. I'll email you some information. Congratulations again, Laura.'

'Thank you,' Laura said before placing the phone back in the cradle. She was on a high and didn't want to talk about Gary, not now and not with Joanna, but thought she'd better get it over with.

She prepared herself for the call as she made herself a cup of tea in the kitchen. Senior Constable Roberts asked her if she was ready to do the missing person's report, and she said she needed a few more minutes, telling him she had one more call to make.

As she blew on the hot tea in her hands, her mind drifted back to the court case. Testifying had been terrifying, but she and Joanna had supported each other.

The defence tried to find holes. They tried to paint Laura as a troubled teen who'd needed professional counselling in the past and Joanna as an unreliable witness, a hell-raiser, fixated on finding anyone to blame for her brothers' deaths. But they failed.

The girls' accounts were rock-solid. As she was being questioned, Laura had kept her eyes focused on the prosecution and defence lawyers, refusing to let her gaze wander to Gary. But she could feel him watching her. When the time came, she turned to him, verifying Gary as the man in the car who'd asked her for directions. When she looked into his eyes, all the dreams, all the old fears washed over her, and it took a long time to stop her hands from shaking after she stepped down. Joanna took a different approach and stared at Gary for the entire time she was on the stand. Her face defiant, Joanna pointed at the man who'd ripped the heart out of her family, identifying him as the driver of the white Toyota Hilux.

Adding weight to the prosecution case was the body they found in the lake. The body they had only discovered so quickly because of Laura and her dream. Dental records confirmed it was Mia, and the wounds to her head were consistent with those inflicted on the Thompson boys and Yvette Berger. Tyre tracks found by the water's edge also matched those on Gary's ute. It strengthened the police case and allowed the Stevens family to bury their daughter and for the town to start to heal. Laura had tried hard for the past year to put the encounter with Gary behind her.

So much had changed.

The farm was no longer theirs. Struggling to stay afloat for years, Jack and Henry had no choice in the end but to sell up after the trial. The old farmhouse and milking sheds had been ripped down, and the property was being subdivided as part of a new housing estate.

Her parents and Yogi now lived on the far south coast of New South Wales, on a ten-acre hobby farm near Bega that kept them occupied in their retirement. Her grandfather, Jack, lived with them. Grace had passed away two months ago from an aggressive cancer. By the time they detected it, the disease had already progressed to her liver. It took her beloved grandmother from them way too soon. Like the rest of the family, Laura couldn't believe Gran was gone.

Her sister, Sarah, had followed her dreams and joined a band with other music students from university. She played keyboards with Waiting for Tomorrow. The group had been discovered through triple j radio's Unearthed competition. They already had a strong following and a string of hits in Australia. The band had just left for a tour of the UK. Sarah was engaged to fellow band member Archie, the bass player she started dating in university, and was busy with her rock-star lifestyle. Despite not seeing each other for months, the sisters were still close and caught up via a video call every week.

Laura's thoughts returned to the news about Gary Wilson. She wondered how Joanna was doing. Her friend had been on her mind since receiving an invitation from her to attend a special ceremony to erect a memorial in honour of the lives taken by Gary at Wallaby Rock.

Arthur and Leo Thompson had campaigned long and hard for it. But Arthur would never get to see his vision realised. He'd passed away only a few weeks after Gary's trial. Laura believed Mr Thompson had never recovered from the loss of his sons. She had often wondered if it was possible to die of a broken heart.

Joanna had been distraught to lose her father, and for a while, Laura worried her friend may spiral out of control, but she'd forgotten how tough Joanna was. After burying her father, her friend sold their house and moved to Wagga Wagga to be closer to her mother's family. She'd met a nice guy and had confided to Laura that she was expecting a child with him. They were planning on getting married next year, once the baby was born. She wanted Laura to be her maid of honour and godmother to her child.

Laura checked the date on the invitation for the memorial, Saturday 25 February 2023. Less than a fortnight away – she'd better call Joanna back, to accept and check how she was doing. She looked up to see Constable Roberts pointing at paperwork on his desk.

'I'll just be a minute,' she replied. Picking up the phone, she dialled Joanna's number. It rang several times before her old friend answered.

'Hi, Joanna. It's Laura,' she said.

'Laura, hey. Hang on a minute, will you?' Joanna said, and Laura heard her talking to someone in the background. 'Sorry. Just had to finish up with a *lovely* customer.' Joanna's sarcasm was clear. She'd picked up a job working in an office for a big agri-business firm in Wagga. She'd told Laura most customers were great, but occasionally you had to deal with men who just liked to tell the 'little woman' how she should do her job.

Laura laughed. 'How's Mark? Did you guys have a nice Christmas?'

'We're good,' said Joanna. 'Thank you so much for the gift. We loved it. By the way, how's your love life? Any hunky boys in blue swept you off your feet yet?'

Laura coughed quickly before answering, 'Ah, no, not yet.' Laura laughed. 'I'm glad you liked the gift. I just wanted to thank you for inviting me to the commemoration. I'd love to come.'

'Perfect. It'll be great to see you. It's been too long.' Joanna's voice sobered. 'Did you hear the news about Gary Wilson? Got knocked off in prison.'

'Yeah, I heard,' Laura replied. 'Are you okay?'

'I am, but I wish he'd suffered more. Damn it. He deserves to be in pain for eternity,' Joanna said, her voice as savage as ever.

They were quiet for a moment until their silence was interrupted by Senior Constable Roberts, who called from across the room, 'C'mon, Constable Murray. We have work to do,' he said loud enough for Joanna to hear.

'Alright, I'm finishing up now,' Laura almost shouted back.

'Sorry, Joanna. I have to go. I'll see you in a couple of weeks. It'll be great to catch up.'

'See you soon, Constable Murray,' Joanna cheekily replied.

Chapter 46 – Laura

At the end of another long day, Laura opened the gate to a narrow side path leading to a granny flat she rented at the back of her uncle's home in Heathcote. Less than forty kilometres from the Sydney CBD, the home backed onto the Royal National Park, where Laura enjoyed the walking trails that wove their way through bushland.

She could hear the noise of the television as she passed the main house before turning the key in the door and letting herself into the small space she called her own. She'd been staying with her uncle since she joined the station at Heathcote and was glad the location was also close to the police dog squad in Menai, southwest of Sydney. As she kicked off her shoes and hung up her uniform, she grabbed a glass of wine and walked to the tiny bathroom. Turning on the taps, she poured pink bubble bath in the tub and switched on her bathtub-soak playlist. As she sank into the warm, perfumed water, she felt some of the stress of the day wash away.

After changing into shorts and a loose top, she padded her way to the kitchen to heat some leftover pasta bake.

As she poured another wine and sat on the couch to enjoy her meal, her mobile rang.

'Laura, it's Mum. I wanted to see how you're doing. We heard the news about Gary Wilson.' Jeannie's voice was laden with concern, and Laura could picture her mother fretting. Jeannie had her on speaker, so she knew her father was somewhere close by, listening in.

'Hi, Mum,' Laura said. 'Don't worry about me. I'm okay, and hi, Dad.'

'Hi, love,' Henry called. 'Are you doing okay?'

'I am, and I don't want you both stressing about me,' Laura replied.

'I can't believe he's gone,' Jeannie chimed in. 'Have you spoken to Joanna? How's she doing?'

'Joanna's fine. If anything, she's a bit disappointed. She wanted him to suffer, for a long time. I think she feels a bit cheated by his death,' Laura confided.

'I can understand that. But he can't hurt anyone ever again, which is good. How's work going? Are you enjoying it still?' her mother probed.

'I am, Mum, and I've got some news. I got accepted into training for the dog squad. It's super competitive, so I'm proud to get this far, especially as I'm only so new to the service. They did say, though, that not everyone makes it through.'

'Oh, Laura, that's wonderful. We'll let your grandfather know. Are you going to the commemoration?' Jeannie asked. 'Joanna sent us an invitation.'

'Yeah, I've already taken that day off work. Will I see you there?'

'Yes, darling, your father and I will be there but not your grandfather. It's … too much for him at the moment. Going back there. Too many memories,' Jeannie said, her voice low.

'I get it,' Laura replied. 'It must be hard. Please give him a big hug from me. But I'll see you and Dad in a couple of weeks then?'

'You will. Take care, sweetheart,' Jeannie said.

'Bye, love,' her father called.

'Bye, Mum and Dad. Love you,' Laura replied.

***

The smell and noise of the suburbs fall away as the familiar chatter and call of birds fill the sky. Smiling, she waves to a carolling magpie flying overhead as she nears the lookout.

Crunching feet on the path signals someone is coming up the track, and she turns to say hello, but no one's there.

Laura keeps walking. There it is again. Someone is definitely behind her, but they are moving carefully, and quietly. Laura steps off the track and takes cover in the trees.

He stoops, head low, examining the ground where her footprints end.

'I know you're there. You think I've gone? That I can't reach you, Laura?' The familiar voice is laughing as he rises, pushing a lock of dirty blond hair from his face as he moves

closer. 'I'm part of you. You'll never be free of me. And I'm not the only one!'

Laura freezes, and all her training evaporates as she stares at the face of the man who has haunted her dreams for so many years.

***

She was panting, drenched in sweat. The doona lay in a mess on the floor.

'Bloody hell,' she yelled to the night. How did she let him get into her head again? She couldn't – wouldn't let him win.

Her mouth was dry, and she padded to the kitchen sink, grabbed a glass, filled it, and gulped the water down. Gripping the bench, she willed herself to clear her head. It was just a dream. It didn't mean anything!

After fixing the bed, she climbed in, turned on the bedside lamp, and opened the book she'd been reading. Forty minutes later, she turned off the light, but it was another hour before she fell into a restless sleep.

Chapter 47 – Laura

The sun beat down on her head, and she realised she'd once again forgotten a hat. Laura stood beside Joanna and her boyfriend, Mark, and her parents and her faithful dog, Yogi, his muzzle tinged with grey, were close by her side. Dressed in plain clothes, Laura cradled a bunch of native Australian flowers in her arms.

After a moving Welcome to Country, the now-retired Senator Leo Thompson stepped forward. He first acknowledged the local Aboriginal people and their connection to the land they were standing on before welcoming the NSW premier, the local federal member of parliament, the state member of parliament, and the mayor.

In the crowd were many faces Laura recognised, including Sergeant Mick Peters, Senior Constable Bob Fowler, and Constable Erica Martin. Erica smiled at Laura over the heads of shuffling people as Leo spoke.

Joanna's uncle addressed the attendees, and media congregated on the side of the road, next to the bridge. Leo acknowledged the tireless efforts of Arthur Thompson in seeking recognition and justice for the murders that occurred in 2020 and during the early days of white settlement. Leo told them to remember the lives taken away too soon, including those of his nephews, Benny and Jordy.

Joanna stood tall and proud but teared up when Leo talked about her father and brothers. Leo paused, eyes locked on his niece.

'We're gathered here today to remember. Remember two young men and two young women whose lives were ripped away.

'Arthur Thompson's sons were murdered at this place, not far from where this memorial stands. So, too, were Yvette Berger and Mia Stevens – two hundred years after the death of an innocent man and a newborn baby. I want you to think about that.

'These brutal acts of violence continue to leave a mark on this country, a scar on this land that will never heal.

'As another, more eloquent, politician, Edmund Burke, once said, 'The only thing necessary for the triumph of evil is for good men to do nothing.' Arthur Thompson didn't stand by and do nothing and neither did his ancestor George Thompson.

'I'd like to ask the premier to unveil the memorial in honour of those who are no longer with us.'

The premier addressed the crowd, thanking the police who searched for the young people who would never come home and all those who helped bring the killer to justice. Cameras flashed as the premier lifted the cloth lying over a large sandstone rock and invited the families of the victims to come forward.

Joanna stepped through the crowd, dodging reporters as she laid a bunch of bright-coloured flowers and a football at the base of the memorial. She was followed by Bernhard Berger and Don Stevens.

On the stone was a plaque with an inscription:

> *This plaque commemorates the memory of the following persons whose lives were taken at this place in 2020.*
>
> *Benjamin (Benny) John Thompson*
> *Jordan (Jordy) Matthew Thompson*
> *Yvette Stefanie Berger (Germany)*
> *Mia Anne Stevens*
>
> *We also remember the lives of convict Michael Murphy and an unnamed baby boy who were killed here in 1822.*
>
> *These deaths have changed this place, the country we call home, forever.*
>
> *Acknowledgement is made of the efforts of members of the New South Wales Police Service, State Emergency Service and local volunteers.*

The ceremony concluded and Laura hugged her friend before making her way through the throng to the memorial. Crouching, she placed her flowers next to Joanna's. She touched the top of the jagged sandstone and ran her fingers over the words on the plaque. She closed her eyes and remembered Arthur, Benny, and Jordy. She said a prayer to Saint Patrick for their souls, and the souls of the others killed by Gary Wilson and Jeremiah Pyke, just like Gran had taught her. She wiped her eyes, stood, and turned back to the crowd to find Erica close behind her.

'Hello, Laura. It's good to see you,' Erica said, giving Laura a swift hug.

'Erica, nice to see you too. I didn't know you'd be here.'

'Mick and Bob told me. I wanted to come.'

'How's the new job in Sydney?' Laura asked, taking in Erica's shiny police badge and spotless uniform.

'I love the task force. Come over one night for dinner; you can meet my new partner, Tony.'

'I didn't know you had a new boyfriend, Erica. You kept that one quiet,' Laura teased.

'Yeah, well, it's still early days, but come over, and I'll fill you in about work, but life's pretty good right now. I love my job, but I don't love Sydney. I'm still a country girl at heart,' she said with a grin.

Erica's time at Wallaby Rock had a significant impact on her and was shaping her career. The two women were good friends and now colleagues. Laura knew Erica had been handpicked to join a new task force that specialised in tracking down missing people and re-investigating cold cases. In a short time, Erica was earning a reputation for getting results, often through unusual investigative methods, and for undertaking complex undercover sting operations.

'Are you enjoying life as a plod?' Erica joked.

Laura laughed. 'I am, but guess what? I got accepted to dog squad training. I start next week!'

'Ah, Laura, that's awesome. It's right up your alley. Congratulations. It's not easy to get into the training squad, especially when you're new. You must have impressed them,' Erica said, and Laura could hear the pride in her mentor's voice. While female officers were now common in the force, the two young women supported each other at every step.

'I'd better get going. I already said hello to your parents and Yogi. Work awaits,' Erica finished before giving Laura another hug and hurrying off to say goodbye to Mick and Bob, who waved her over.

Laura rubbed the rough sandstone edges of the memorial once more before returning to her family and Joanna.

Acknowledgements

They say it takes a village to raise a child, and at times, this story has been like raising a troublesome teenager. Just when I thought I had a handle on what to do and where to go, there were mood swings and tantrums as my child, just like Laura Murray, struggled to find its own identity and voice. But the journey was worth it.

Thank you to my village. To those wonderful individuals who believed in me, listened to my woes, and encouraged me to keep going.

First, I'd like to thank Shayne, my husband and my rock, who allowed me the freedom to be creative and follow this path. To my parents, John and Shirley, and my sister, Sonia, who've stood steadfastly by my side – thank you for your unwavering support and valuable insights.

This story would not have seen the light of day without my children: Dylan (who came up with the title for this book) and Lauren (who pushed me to delve deeper into the minds of my characters). Their advice and critical feedback kept me grounded.

I cannot thank enough my lifelong friend and amazing editor, Sharon Phillips, who patiently reviewed draft after draft, guided me when I was unsure which direction to take, and held my hand through the 'long tail'.

To my Aunty Marg, a proud Yorta Yorta woman, thank you for your support and good counsel. You are, and will always be, my beautiful aunty.

Thank you Lisa Portolan for pointing me in the right direction as I tried to navigate this crazy world of publishing. Special thanks to Jenn McLeod for your early assessment that made *Bad Country* a much better read and for your encouragement to keep growing as a writer. To CH, thank you for helping me to keep it real.

A big thank you to the crew who helped to finesse the final product, Daina Lindeman and Pheonix Raig for their editing prowess and to Amanda Bennett at Rubi Creations Digital for the fantastic cover design. To Fiona Smith at Contempo Publishing, my sincere and heartful gratitude for taking a chance on me and for guiding me through each step. Without you, *Bad Country* would still only exist as a file on my laptop.

Thank you to the network of fabulous authors I've had the pleasure of listening to or chatting with, including those in the Eurobodalla Writers, ACT Writers (Marion), the CYA Conferences, and the Sydney Writers' Festival. Your experiences inspired me to stick with it when self-doubt set in.

To my furry grandson, Banjo, thank you for keeping me company in the back room.

Finally, to my cousins who endured late-night scary stories when we were growing up – I hope you enjoyed this.